THE DEMON OF DARTMOOR

THE
DEMON
OF
DARTMOOR

Paul Halter

TRANSLATED BY TOM MEAD

NO EXIT PRESS

First published as *Le Diable de Dartmoor* in 1993 by Librairie des Champs-Élysées, Paris

This paperback translation published in the UK in 2026 by No Exit Press,
an imprint of Bedford Square Publishers Ltd,
London, UK

noexit.co.uk
@noexitpress

ISBN
978-1-83501-350-2 (Paperback)
978-1-83501-351-9 (eBook)

2 4 6 8 10 9 7 5 3 1

Typeset in 11.25 on 14pt Garamond MT Pro
by Avocet Typeset, Bideford, Devon, EX39 2BP
Printed and bound in Great Britain by
CPI Group (UK) Ltd, Croydon CR0 4YY

The manufacturer's authorised representative in the EU for
product safety is Easy Access System Europe, Mustamäe tee 50,
10621 Tallinn, Estonia
gpsr.requests@easproject.com

For Jacques Baudou, Jean-Jacques Schléret and Jean-Paul Schweighaeuser, three Alsatian specialists in the murder mystery.
PH

1

Invisible Hands

Lost in the wild expanse of Dartmoor is the tiny village of Stapleford, where the church clock had just struck half-past eleven. The clutch of houses around it seemed to huddle closer; summer was drawing to an end, and a nighttime chill was creeping in.

Among the few windows still lit was the study of Professor Victor Sitwell. The wrinkles on his brow suggested a contemplative nature, as did the blue eyes peering through *pince-nez*, unblinking. The professor's conscientiousness, erudition and overall demeanour were highly regarded at the school in Tavistock where he taught philosophy. He was admired by colleagues, students and parents alike. Such unanimity is a rare and beautiful thing, and this esteem was shared – for the most part – by the residents of Stapleford. He was generally considered to be the village's leading intellect *and* its most generous benefactor. He was always on hand to assist those in distress, and never failed to leave at least a ten-shilling note in the collection plate at Sunday service.

That evening he sat at his desk as usual. Unusually, though, he had neither pen nor paper to hand. Anyone who knew him would have noticed immediately that something was troubling him. He was about to retire for the night when he heard a knock at the front door. He glanced at the clock. A visitor at this hour? His annoyance quickly turned to apprehension.

On the doorstep he found John and Betty, local youngsters of around seventeen or eighteen. They looked deeply embarrassed and apologised for the lateness of their visit. Victor Sitwell reassured them and showed them through to his study. It took a little while longer, though, for them to get to the point.

'You must understand, Professor, that Betty and I can't let our parents find out we've been… *meeting* in secret. We'd never hear the end of it. So we can never tell them about what we saw last night, especially considering *when* and *where* we saw it,' John stammered, blushing slightly. 'They'd know right away that Betty and I… that me and Betty…'

The professor gave him an encouraging nod, and he paused to compose himself. 'We've spent the whole day fretting,' he added, more calmly now, 'then we thought of *you*, sir.'

'You always know the right thing to do,' Betty interjected.

'If we hadn't seen the light in the window, we never would have knocked, of course…'

'And if my parents found out, they'd never let me see John again…'

'You do understand, don't you, sir?'

Victor Sitwell cleared his throat, silencing them both. 'I understand the situation perfectly. You care for one another, you wish to meet in private, and you're anxious that your parents do not find out. However, the cat would be out of the bag if you were to report this mysterious "event" – presumably a very serious one – that you witnessed last night. Am I correct? Excellent. Then you have no need to worry, I will preserve your secret to the best of my ability. However, before we proceed further you had better explain the nature of this "event" you witnessed.'

Neither of them could meet his gaze.

'You won't believe us, sir,' said John.

'It's quite unbelievable,' Betty added, 'and yet…'

'We did wonder if we might be hallucinating, of course… but

the two of us saw the same thing at the same time, so that's impossible.'

'It made us think of some of the strange stories they tell around here… like the death of that young lady at the big house just outside the village… something Manor…'

'Trerice Manor,' Sitwell supplied, disconcerted by the mention of this long-ago tragedy. Had they witnessed something connected to that mysterious incident? If so, what?

'Please, let's get to the point,' he said gently.

John glanced at his companion, gulped, then began to speak. 'A girl was pushed off the edge of a cliff… but there was nobody anywhere near her.'

In the silence that followed, the professor sat perfectly still, not taking his eyes off his two visitors. 'Go on,' he finally said.

'It was around this time – that is, close to midnight. Betty and I had been up on Wish Tor for about fifteen minutes…'

Wish Tor… Victor Sitwell now understood the youngsters' reticence. There could be little doubt as to what they were doing there at that hour. Wish Tor was a popular spot for lovers; beautiful both by day and night, but especially at night, by the glow of the moon and the blanket of stars. It was an impressive granite ridge above a thin stream that babbled its way towards the village, less than a mile below. The rock was of a rather curious shape, vaguely reminiscent of the Sphinx. Some locals likened it to a wild beast, poised to pounce, its imperious features gazing down over the tumbling waters.

One could spend hours up there, listening to the water coursing between rocks against the splendid backdrop of Dartmoor; its ragged crests and gentle slopes, dotted with oaks and firs. The place had an extraordinary atmosphere; a combination of profound serenity and deep melancholy that was especially noticeable at dusk, when the recumbent sun blazed just below the horizon, hidden from view by the hills and peaks. By night, though the landscape was largely shrouded in darkness, its ancient magic was more powerful than ever. Few young couples could resist the musical sound of the stream, which summoned them like a siren song.

Wish Tor acquired its name because of a supposed propensity for granting them. At its summit was a plateau scattered with rocks and a small cave, ideal for lovers sheltering from a storm. John began to explain this to Victor Sitwell, amid various awkward circumlocutions. 'That's where we were when we heard footsteps. It was a girl coming up the path, heading in our direction. The moon was beautiful and bright, so we could see her perfectly. She couldn't see *us*, of course, because we were in the shadow of the cave. She was humming to herself quite happily, which seemed rather odd. You see, she was quite alone, although she acted as though there was someone at her side. We thought she might be meeting someone and had just got there early – we'd been up there for quite a while, and would have seen anyone else arrive. She walked past the cave and we'd just lost sight of her when we heard her call out, "Hello? Where are you?"

'Betty and I just looked at each other, wondering if there might be somebody hiding up there somehow. But the girl called out a few more times, always in that same cheery voice, as though someone was playing a trick on her. We slipped out of the cave to get a better view.'

John glanced at his sweetheart, inviting her to resume the tale. Betty nodded gravely. 'She was on the edge of the cliff, about twelve yards away from us. The moon was hidden by clouds, but we could still see her quite clearly. The girl, I mean. There was no one standing anywhere near her. Was there, John? And she called out one last time, "Hey, where are you?" then turned away from us, looking down towards the village. That's when something pushed her from behind, and she went tumbling over the edge... I screamed...'

'Pushed from behind? And there was nobody else there?' exclaimed Sitwell, turning to John for confirmation.

The young man nodded. 'I know it's hard to believe, but it was as if she'd been pushed by… a pair of invisible hands. She didn't stumble by accident. And she didn't jump. She reached forward, hands spread out, trying to save herself – just as if someone was pushing her in the back. Do you see what I mean, Professor? Only there was no one else there!'

After a long, uncomfortable silence, Sitwell shook his head with a reproving look. 'I rather think you two are spinning a yarn. How can you be certain you weren't seeing things? Did you even hear the girl scream? Or the thud of a body hitting the ground below?'

'Yes! Well, no,' John stammered. 'Betty screamed just as the girl went over the edge, so that was all we could hear.'

'And what did you do then? Headed down towards the stream, I presume, at the foot of Wish Tor?'

'We retraced our steps back down the Tor, but we didn't stop at the stream. Betty was scared to death and I… well, I wasn't all that keen either. So we went home.'

Sitwell gave a shrug. 'I doubt you would have found anything anyway. I'm quite convinced you were both tormented by a guilty conscience, which caused you to see things that weren't there. After all, no one has disappeared from the village since—'

He froze, sitting in silence for several long seconds.

'Is something the matter, sir?' asked John cautiously.

'The girl… this girl… did you recognise her?'

'I'm not sure, but Betty thinks it was Constance.'

'Constance Kent?'

'I think so,' said Betty, nodding vigorously.

Sitwell closed his eyes. 'My God,' he said, 'I was just thinking about this before you got here, but it slipped my mind when you came in. I was at the Red Lion earlier this evening, and

Constance's father came in at around nine o'clock looking for his daughter. She'd been working at the inn the previous day, and he assumed she had spent the night there. But the landlord told him she went home and he hadn't seen her since.'

2

The Search

BY FIVE-THIRTY THE FOLLOWING MORNING, STAPLEFORD WAS aglow in the otherworldly light of dawn, a heavy mist drifting in from the stream. Three men busied themselves on the stone bridge across the water, scanning the surface with their torches. Their search had brought them all the way to the foot of Wish Tor and back again.

Among them was Dr Thomas Grant, the least talkative of the three. It might seem that the unceremonious wake-up call was to blame for his sour mood. However, this wasn't the case; he'd been in his particular profession for thirty years and was quite used to early mornings. He cared for his fellow villagers with the utmost skill and dedication, but the warmth of his personality was his greatest asset – more so than any prescription. All his patients agreed that the mere sight of his plump figure and kindly smile at their bedside was sufficient to improve their condition.

No, his sullen demeanour was the result of the shock he had suffered when Victor Sitwell came knocking on his door with that strange story some forty-five minutes earlier.

Likewise Basil Hawkins, a stocky fellow in his thirties (but who looked at least ten years older) made no effort to conceal his prevailing mood. Unlike the doctor, though, he was not accustomed to venturing out at the crack of dawn. With his wild black hair, ruddy complexion and shabby clothing he looked precisely what he was: an alcoholic who had ceased to care for his appearance. His days were divided into three unequal parts: poaching, gardening, and drinking at the Red Lion. This latter activity took up the most generous portion of his time. He lodged in a small shed belonging to a local farmer, sleeping on bales of hay – an arrangement secured for him thanks to the intervention of Victor Sitwell, who wasted no time in hiring him as a gardener. This occupation took up only a few afternoons per week, but the Sitwells were seemingly satisfied with his work.

No one knew where he had come from, nor did they bother to ask any more. He'd been part of the village scenery for almost ten years. It was practically impossible to imagine an evening at the Red Lion without his boisterous good cheer. The landlord, George Crawford, would have been very sorry to see him go. And in spite of his precarious living arrangements, Hawkins seemed to be one of the happiest men in Stapleford – particularly as he stumbled home each evening. Dr Grant thought so, anyway, which is why he was a frequent drinking companion – albeit in moderation. Curiously, Basil Hawkins's most faithful comrade was Professor Sitwell, who stopped in for a tipple almost every evening.

This friendship between the local drunk and the village intellectual had caused some intrigue at first, but even this had faded after a while. Besides, it was well-known that Victor liked a drink. It didn't affect him in the same way as Basil, but it often induced him to make grand disquisitions on all manner of subjects, which the other regulars warmly applauded – though they rarely understood a word.

For now, though, no one was thinking about those warm, cosy evenings at the Red Lion. Victor Sitwell stood with his coat collar turned up about his ears, his features drawn. The beam from his torch ran over the surface of the water.

He had not slept at all the previous night. After sending the two youngsters home – with a promise not to say a word for the time being – he had sat back at his desk to reflect on the matter. He concluded that the best course of action was to try to ascertain the accuracy of their account by locating the body. Basil had proved difficult to rouse, his sluggishness matched by the stench of his breath. Dr Thomas Grant, however, answered his door promptly and joined the meagre search party without a fuss.

Shortly before five o'clock, the three men equipped themselves with flashlights and ventured up towards Wish Tor. They allowed themselves two hours at the most for the search; after that, their activities were bound to be noticed.

So far, though, they had turned up nothing. In spite of the lack of illumination, they were quite convinced there was no body in the stream at the foot of the Tor. An object had briefly caught their attention, drifting amid the eddies, but it was only a wooden stick.

Recent rainfall had raised the water level, so it was quite capable of carrying a body away. With that in mind, the three searchers walked slowly alongside the stream, limiting themselves to a cursory investigation. The idea that the two teenagers had been mistaken was beginning to take hold – particularly in Sitwell's mind. But a remark from Basil Hawkins dampened his optimism: 'With this current, she could be miles away by now. Remember Eliza Gold last year… she turned up a long, long way from here.'

'Please, Basil,' snapped Sitwell, 'this has nothing to do with Eliza Gold.'

After that, there was a silence, broken only when Sitwell met the curious gaze of Dr Grant. 'Nothing? How can you say that? Eliza Gold was twenty – she disappeared, then turned up drowned three days later, her body all covered with bruises. And now here we are, barely a year on, looking for a young woman of the same age, who also mysteriously disappeared on a summer evening. How can you say there's no connection?' He spoke with uncharacteristic vehemence before continuing, 'Forgive me, Victor, but I find that remark surprising, given your professional interest in logic.'

'No one believed me. Not one of them,' murmured Basil Hawkins, his gaze fixed on the pink and gold light beyond the distant hills. 'The horse. And the headless horseman. No one wanted to believe me.' He turned abruptly to Sitwell, declaring, 'And the cards! What about the cards they found on her?'

A deck of playing cards had been found in Eliza's pocket – this much was true. Completely waterlogged, of course, after being submerged as long as it had. And it was also true that Basil Hawkins made a claim the day after Eliza's disappearance that he had seen a headless horseman, riding off into the sky at the presumed hour she was taken.

But he'd been drinking heavily on the night in question – he never denied it. He couldn't even remember where exactly this visitation had occurred, though he remained resolute in his claim that he saw a real horse with a headless rider, who came galloping past him before soaring up towards the heavens. He was quite convinced its appearance was connected to the missing girl, and that she would not be found – at least, not alive. Someone else speculated that they would likely find a pack of cards in the vicinity of her disappearance. And two days later, Eliza Gold turned up dead in the water – with a pack of cards on her person.

Her body had been in the water for about three days, neatly corresponding to the last time she was seen in public, at the inn. She'd been in excellent spirits at the time, which seemed to rule out suicide. She was also covered with bruises and various other wounds, not to mention broken bones. However, this wasn't all that surprising, bearing in mind the likelihood that her body had been tossed back and forth between rocks by the cascading waters. The coroner's jury returned a verdict of accidental death, but this did not prevent the circulation of certain ugly rumours.

Sitwell drew a deep breath before declaring, 'Calm down, fellows. This isn't the time to succumb to hysteria.' He turned to the doctor. 'You're right, Thomas. And, of course, I haven't forgotten what happened last year. But it's still premature to jump to conclusions. As for the horseman, Basil… well. The less said about that the better. That's not a judgement, all I'm saying is that it's best not to talk about it for the time being. Do you understand, Basil?'

Hawkins stared blankly at the professor for a few seconds, then nodded.

At that moment, the doctor's expression changed. He had just placed his flashlight on the ground for a moment to free up his hands. Its beam suddenly illuminated a roiling, bronze-coloured mass below the surface of the water. It was a woman's head of hair.

Within minutes, the three men hauled ashore the body which had lain suspended between two jagged rocks. It was indeed Constance Kent, and she was in a similar state to Eliza Gold when she was found the previous year. Haunted by their discovery, they spent some time gazing down at the unfortunate body, all bruised and broken.

Sitwell was the first to examine the surrounding area with his torch, and that's when he spotted something unusual, clinging to a patch of moss. He approached it slowly, his companions close behind.

It was a playing card.

3

History Repeats Itself

I T WAS EARLY EVENING, AND BASIL HAWKINS sat alone in a corner of the Red Lion. The place was unusually quiet. It had been a close, muggy sort of day, and the half-open lattice window behind him was the only source of cool air. He looked at the pair of empty tankards on the table in front of him before ambling over to the bar, where George Crawford, a burly chap with thick sideburns, stood cleaning glasses against a backdrop of bottles. In front of him gleamed a parade of copper taps, positively bursting with beer.

Basil's face lit up when the door opened and in walked Professor Sitwell. Within a minute, the two men were sitting at the table, a pair of fresh, foaming tankards in front of them.

'You seem distracted, sir,' said Basil between sips.

'Distracted? Dear fellow, I am *furious*. I cannot fathom how the human race has survived as long as it has with only selfishness, aggression and ingratitude to sustain it. I'd always thought the McKenzies were a decent sort. After all I've done for them – their son would never have passed his exams without my assistance! – this is how they repay me. They won't allow the gypsies to settle on their land. And they have an entire barn, lying empty! The Warrens, the Crooks and the Davises have all taken a turn, but the McKenzies simply refuse…'

'But… aren't the gypsies quite happy where they are, in their caravans by the bridge?'

Victor Sitwell gave an exasperated sigh. 'Basil, I *promised* to help them find a new settlement on a farm. I *promised* them. And now I'm made to look a fool! I cannot bear the McKenzies and their ilk… wicked, selfish people!'

'Well, Professor, not everyone can be like you. I can't think of many people who would have looked after *me* as you did…'

'Let's change the subject, shall we, Basil?' said the professor with a weary smile. 'Besides, Florence and I are more than happy with your work; I hardly consider it "looking after" you. Anyway, let's not talk about it any more. Another beer?' He turned towards the bar: 'George, two more!'

It was not George Crawford who brought over the next round of drinks, but Annie Crook, a pretty sixteen-year-old brunette who'd been living under the Crawfords' roof for five years or so. She was only eleven, and quite terrified, when the professor first brought her into the pub, explaining that she had lost her parents, who were local farmers. Since George and Alice Crawford were a childless couple, they had gladly taken her in. And they had never once regretted it.

Though she was understandably shy at first, Annie soon made herself useful, taking care of the stables with great enthusiasm and assisting Alice around the place – particularly on busy weekends when a sudden influx of tourists stopped off at the inn en route to Tavistock.

Basil watched her go before leaning forward to confide, 'I think *she* owes you a debt of gratitude, too.'

'I only did my duty, Basil. But, as you rightly point out, it seems that some people don't have the same idea of neighbourliness as I do.'

Basil stared silently into the middle distance.

The professor frowned. 'What are you thinking about, Basil?'

'In a few days it'll be September again. A whole year since we found the Kent girl. And those playing cards…'

Sitwell did not need to be reminded. He immediately saw the red hair rippling against the current, the body lying cold on the shore, the playing card close by, and then another…

By daybreak, they had collected almost an entire deck which had been scattered across the pasture near their gruesome discovery. As with Eliza Gold, investigators returned a verdict of accidental death. Sitwell reported the tale told by the two young lovers, but the police officer in charge – a local man, and a longtime friend – had not included it in his report. Nor did he mention the discovery of the playing cards. He was equally reticent about another statement received from Annie Crook, who had been with the victim just before she headed up to Wish Tor.

'So she was working behind the bar till eleven?' the police officer asked.

'Yes,' Annie replied, 'she worked every weekend because of—'

'I know about that, the landlord told me. What I'm interested in is the time. Did she leave at eleven o'clock exactly?'

'Yes. Well… give or take ten minutes or so. I'd just gone up to my room, and I saw her from the window. She was humming to herself. Like I said, she was in a cheery mood all evening. And she was walking towards Wish Tor when she stopped near a tree. I could see her speaking to someone, but I couldn't tell who it was. Then she carried on her way. She was still talking – even laughing – but there was no one with her. I'm quite sure of that.'

Victor Sitwell, Basil Hawkins and Dr Grant had all been present when Annie made her statement, and now Basil took the opportunity to recall it to the professor. Sitwell removed his *pince-nez*, unfolded a handkerchief to dab the sweat from his forehead, then said, 'We've already discussed this, Basil. There's nothing more to be done about it. Better just to try and forget. Anyway, I had better leave you now. I have some paperwork to complete. And right on cue, here's Thomas!'

Dr Grant took Sitwell's place at the table and ordered a round, which Annie brought over.

'The chrysalis has yielded a beautiful butterfly,' he observed cheerfully once she was gone. 'But for heaven's sake, what on earth is she doing *here*, with only old fogies for company all year round? What say you, Basil?'

'Well, I reckon…' Basil paused, watching Annie make her way across the rapidly filling bar. The room was getting warmer, the conversations louder, and the cigarette smoke thicker. 'I reckon you're right. She's always had a kind of sadness about her. But these last few days – and tonight especially – she seems to have cheered up no end.'

'Indeed,' said the doctor. 'I wonder what's behind it?'

With that, Dr Grant got up and bade Basil a good evening. Finding himself alone at the table again, Basil headed for the bar to order another beer, which he downed in a single gulp. He then looked at the man to his right, a young shepherd named David Lynder. Lynder was handsome, but reserved. At that moment, he could not take his eyes off Annie.

Basil sang the chorus of an old love song, but David did not join in. 'The fool,' thought Basil. 'Standing here like a dummy when it's plain to see he's head-over-heels.'

Soon afterwards, Basil returned to his seat. The room had begun to spin, and he almost collapsed onto the bench. Then he glanced around and noticed that Lynder was nowhere in sight. He must have gone to check on his flock. After all, Annie was still here.

'Strange,' thought Basil, 'I've never seen her like this before. She's grinning, and humming as she carries around that tray of hers…'

He didn't leave until closing time. As he was having some difficulty moving without assistance, George Crawford helped him out to the street, whereupon he insisted that he be left to walk home in peace.

Within minutes, he was on the path up to Wish Tor. Realising his mistake, he doubled back – however, this caused him to topple over sideways and into a thicket. His head was spinning, and the moon seemed to waver and ripple. That's when he heard the laughter. A light, melodious sound. He peered at his blurred surroundings, finally spotting the silhouette of a young woman coming up the path. She was laughing and chatting… and yet she was entirely alone. There was no one ahead of her, or behind, or beside.

Annie? Yes, it had to be Annie. But what on earth was she doing up here at this hour? Basil's mind, still brimming with booze, began to wander. Eliza Gold had been in excellent spirits the night the headless rider came for her… Constance Kent was cheerful, too, the night she disappeared, laughing and chatting to a person who wasn't there, just before a pair of invisible hands shoved her over the edge…

And now here was young Annie, gossiping away to nobody as she ambled up to Wish Tor…

Basil opened his mouth to say something, to call out a warning. He wanted to tell her she was in danger, that she'd end up dead in the water like the other two… But he couldn't muster a single word. It was as if his vocal cords were paralysed.

Meanwhile, Annie made her way cheerfully towards the summit.

4

The Demon

Victor Sitwell pushed open the gate and ambled towards the beautiful stone residence at the other end of the long drive. It was undoubtedly the most opulent home in Stapleford. The elaborate topiaries and exquisitely manicured lawn were among the best-kept in the area. And then there were the rosebushes: Victor's pride and joy. He was the only one permitted to care for them; he treated them with almost paternal affection and often joked with Basil that the gardener would be sacked on the spot if he dared touch a single petal. No one but Victor had touched those rosebushes ever since he first moved into the house after his marriage to Florence.

Florence was an only child, and had not only inherited her parents' property but also an extensive portfolio of valuable securities. These were now managed – profitably – by the professor. After surveying his domain with some satisfaction, Victor Sitwell entered the house and went through to the drawing room, where he and Florence practised the daily ritual of afternoon tea.

Though they were roughly the same age, Florence looked considerably younger. Her delicate features and excellent taste kept her remarkably fashionable, even after all these years.

'Any sign of her?' she asked anxiously.

'None. She'll be long gone by now. The stream will have carried her to the Tamar, and then most likely out to sea. It's been nearly a week, and all these rainstorms we've been having…'

'I spoke to Basil this afternoon.'

'Ah. Basil.'

'If only he wouldn't drink so much. He was positively sloshed the night she disappeared.'

'Believe me, nobody regrets it more than Basil himself. He's quite aware that if he'd been in his right mind he might have caught up to the girl, or at least warned her, instead of passing out in a ditch.'

'Now, tell me Victor, what do you think of that story of his?'

'I think he shouldn't have let himself get so drunk. And while I know he's quite incapable of lying, I doubt we can take his testimony at face value. But then, there's also the matter of those playing cards we found nearby…'

'First Eliza Gold,' Florence commenced, 'then Constance Kent last year… and now Annie, last seen by Basil heading up to Wish Tor. Personally, I believe him. Someone was with Annie that night. The same person who was with Constance and Eliza when they disappeared. The same person who threw each of them into the water.'

Sitwell met his wife's gaze. 'Someone? But who? Or rather, *what?* After all, each of the witnesses seems to think we're dealing with an invisible man.'

'I don't understand you, Victor. Sometimes you're the most open-minded person I know, and other times you are completely closed off.'

'It's not a matter of open-mindedness, my dear. All I'm saying is that we ought to be cautious with any tale told by a drunkard — particularly when the events in question took place in the dark.'

'The tragedy at Trerice Manor didn't happen in the dark.'

Victor Sitwell set his teacup on the table with a clatter. 'What are you getting at, Florence? I can tell you have something else on your mind.'

She glanced down for a moment, then looked back at her husband. 'Let's just say I have my own ideas. Besides, the rumour mill has been hard at work, as you can imagine. All this talk of a *demon*...'

'Please, my dear! Let's not talk of it any more, I beg you.'

'All I'm doing is reporting what I hear in the village. Whether or not the fellow can make himself invisible, I'm quite convinced we are dealing with a creature from the depths of hell who looks perfectly normal like you or me. But there's something else these disappearances have in common which has been neglected by most, though Basil himself was quick to point it out. Eliza, Constance and Annie were all in excellent spirits in the hours before their disappearance.'

'Indeed,' Sitwell said thoughtfully, 'and what do you conclude from that?'

'I spoke to Basil at some length. I don't think there can be any doubt about it. Each girl was acting as if she were in love.'

There was a silence, and then the professor remarked, 'And if I understand you correctly, you think it is the same "lover" in each case? Some young and mysterious seducer in the village...?'

'Who steals the hearts of young girls, then hurls them from Wish Tor into the water below. But there's no reason to believe we're dealing with a *young* man necessarily. Whatever mask this demon wears, it is clearly a very good one.'

5

A Jaunt Across Dartmoor

TOWARDS THE END OF THE FOLLOWING SUMMER, villagers began each morning by anxiously scanning the surface of the restless waters that run through Stapleford. But there was nothing to be found. Moreover, no young woman from the village – or any of the surrounding villages – was reported missing that year. Nor in any of the following five years. Life gradually returned to normal, and the names Eliza Gold, Constance Kent and Annie Crook seldom arose in conversation any more. They became the stuff of tragic legend, like the heroines of an old folk song.

The air of trepidation and suspicion that lingered over Stapleford eventually dissipated. By the mid-1930s, Dartmoor was once again a peaceful and beautiful beacon for visitors from all over the country. Among these visitors were a young couple who approached from Moretonhampstead in a sporty coupé.

The man behind the wheel was about thirty. Though he was English, he had a continental way about him. Broad-shouldered and slim-hipped, Nigel Manson's skin was tanned, he had wavy black hair and dark, deep-set eyes. But when he smiled, a boyish dimple formed at the corner of his mouth.

His looks appealed to women of all ages – and he knew just how to use them. This had helped his career immeasurably. After several years with a theatrical troupe in Canada, where he had begun to make a name for himself, he was now back in

England at last. And while his career in the West End was only just beginning, the press was unanimous: a promising future lay ahead of this gifted young actor. But he had another reason to consider himself the happiest man alive: only three weeks earlier he had married the beautiful young woman who currently occupied the passenger seat.

Mrs Manson was a little younger than her husband. Her smooth, porcelain-skinned features were framed by silky blonde hair that tumbled playfully about her slender shoulders. She had an air of delicacy, rather like a frightened doe, which never fails to awaken the protective instinct in red-blooded males.

After their honeymoon in the Mediterranean, the young couple were on their way to Helen's home town of Torquay.

'I think you should have headed straight for the coast,' Helen remarked, gazing round at the landscape.

'Why? This place is rather pretty, don't you think?'

'Certainly, but at this rate I doubt we'll get there by nightfall.'

Since passing through Exeter, Nigel had been obliged to reduce his speed considerably. The roads were narrow and patterned with potholes, not to mention frequent and unpredictable curves, often hidden by greenery or the glare of the sun.

'But we're in no rush. We've got all the time in the world. Take a look around you, Mrs. Manson. Isn't it magnificent?'

Helen smiled at him, and they both admired the natural beauty as they drove. They passed through a canopy of foliage, but the road was still narrow and winding, lined with drystone walls and overgrown with ivy. The further they travelled from Moretonhampstead, the more melancholic the countryside became; vaster and emptier, though no less remarkable. The fern-covered slopes and granite-topped hills formed a ragged line against the sky.

'What's magnificent to me, Nigel, is the way you navigate these roads. Even with the map in my hand I haven't a clue where we're going. It's as if you know the landscape like the back of your hand.'

Nigel answered after a brief pause, 'Well, I do know the area a little.'

'A little? What do you mean? You know, Nigel, it *can* be rather tiresome having to drag every word out of you…'

'I've been here once or twice before, that's all.'

'Well, I'm not just talking about that. We've known each other six months, and now I'm your wife, but it feels as though I only know as much about you as the newspapers.'

'The *Daily Mirror* ran an article about my time in Canada. If you'd read that…'

'I'm not talking about Canada either. I'm talking about *this* country, and the years you spent here.'

'I already told you: I lived with a great-uncle of mine near Bristol until I turned eighteen.'

'There — do you see? A single sentence to sum up eighteen years of existence!'

'But what else do you want to know? He was the only family I had. Surely you don't want me to bore you with every little detail of that abominable boarding school?'

This moment of tension between the newlyweds did not last. In less than half an hour they were once again enjoying the sweet intoxication of one another's company, as well as the captivating beauty of the landscape. The horizon was ablaze in the setting sun, and purple streaks of twilight were creeping in. The irregular rocky outline of the hills accentuated the fantastical nature of the surroundings. Nigel Manson was greatly impressed by those granite spurs — there was one in particular that caught his eye: Wish Tor.

'Isn't it superb?' he said. 'I absolutely must take some photographs.'

This was no sooner said than done. He pulled the car over at the roadside, and within seconds the young Mrs Manson was posing against the silhouetted hill. Nigel snapped a few pictures, then handed the camera to his wife. 'My turn. Here, take a picture of me in front of that wall there. Or better yet, I'll sit on it so you can get me in frame. Careful! You nearly dropped the camera! It cost a small fortune, you know.'

Of all the bothersome habits a young husband might possess, Nigel's obsession with photography was the one that had surprised Helen the most. He never went outside without a camera – he owned half a dozen, which he displayed proudly in his study. He had a particular predilection for landscapes and – naturally enough – pictures of Helen. Though she considered this fairly normal, she was nonetheless flattered. But it was his obsessive desire to have his *own* picture taken that she found somewhat troubling. He could not snap a picture of her without requesting that she take one of him in return. He tended to favour a relaxed pose against an unusual – even precarious – background, like the drystone wall on which he currently lounged.

Once this ritual was complete, they took to the road. But it wasn't long before Nigel was again drawing the car to a halt. This time his eye was caught by a Gothic Revival-style two-storey house, hidden by overgrown vegetation and snared by iron railings. A sign on the gate, which was partly concealed by ivy, read FOR SALE.

Nigel climbed out of the car and pushed open the gate, which eventually yielded amid creaks and wails of protest. He stood staring at the imposing residence, which was barely visible at the end of the long drive.

Helen came over to join him. 'Don't tell me you're interested in this dump?'

'Dump? It looks pretty solid to me.'

'I… find it rather sinister,' said Helen, peering at the grey building which seemed to lurk in that tangle of greenery. 'Surely you're not thinking of buying it?'

Nigel merely shrugged. 'I doubt I could afford it at present.'

'Buy it?' said a voice from behind the couple. 'You're interested in buying? After all this time? It's been on the market for a good long while.'

They turned and saw an old man in a peaked cap, leaning against a cane. 'I'm from the village down that way...' he pointed towards the tip of a church tower a mile or so further down the road. 'Mind you, I reckon you could get a good deal for the place. I reckon the owner would let you have it for a third of what it's worth.'

The Mansons exchanged a puzzled look, then Nigel said, 'Why would he do that?'

The old man gave a sneer. 'You're obviously not from round here. This house – Trerice Manor, it's called – has a bit of a reputation. Has done ever since a woman was pushed down the stairs by an invisible man.'

'An invisible man?' repeated Nigel. 'But why would she—?'

'Well, it wasn't *her* that said it, of course, on account of the fact her skull was smashed when she hit the ground. But it was an invisible man, all right! There were plenty of witnesses. I can tell you're interested in the story. If you've got ten minutes, I'll be happy to tell you all about it.'

In fact, it took him over fifteen minutes to recount the tragedy, but the couple remained fascinated all the same.

'You know,' he concluded, 'that isn't the only mystery surrounding this house. But I'd better be getting on now – I hope I haven't put you off the place.'

By the time he had disappeared from view at a bend in the road, Helen was in her husband's arms. 'That ghost story has given me a real chill.'

'Not a ghost, darling. An invisible man. There's a difference.'

Intrigued by the earnestness in his voice, she turned and looked at him. 'You sound strange, Nigel. What are you thinking about?'

'I've just had an idea, darling. A fantastic idea.'

6

"The Invisible Man"

THE EYES OF THE TWO MEN WANDERED towards the table, and the curious contraption atop it. The younger man looked almost hypnotised by the blue liquid swirling in the still, which trickled out into a glass beaker, bubbling and frothing. After letting it cool for a moment, he grabbed the beaker and offered it to his companion, whose face was stricken with terror.

'Courage, Alfred. Drink up, there's a good fellow.'

'Sir, are you entirely sure that.,.'

'I assure you that you will not experience the slightest discomfort. It will be completely painless.'

'That's not what I meant, sir. What I mean is, are you entirely sure I will go back to the way I was before?'

'Naturally. Do you see that red bottle over there? A couple of spoonfuls of that and you'll be completely visible again. Besides, Alfred, how could you possibly imagine I would conduct an experiment on you if I were not completely certain of its success?'

'In that case, sir – why conduct the experiment at all?'

'A simple demonstration, my dear Alfred. Nothing more nor less than that. Very well – please drink the contents of the beaker!'

'A demonstration? But sir, why on earth do you wish to demonstrate something of which you are already convinced?'

'The demonstration is not for me, Alfred, but for you.'

'Forgive me, sir, but why don't *you* drink the liquid? Would that not be more logical?'

'Alfred, if you don't drink the stuff immediately, you may consider yourself dismissed.'

'Please, sir…'

'I shall not repeat myself again. Drink the liquid. I'm sure you're aware that I could find a dozen candidates to replace you within the hour if I so wished. And you can bet they'd be willing to drink ten glasses of this stuff if I asked them to!'

The servant steeled himself, gulped, and grabbed the beaker. He closed his eyes, then drained it in one go. Immediately, he looked uneasy. His knees trembled and a cloud of smoke appeared around him, swallowing him entirely.

By the time the smokescreen had faded, Alfred was gone.

'Alfred, it works!' the master cried. 'It works! It's wonderful! Alfred, are you still there?'

The valet's voice emerged from the very spot from which he had disappeared. 'I'm here, sir. And may I say, sir, you seem rather surprised at the result of the experiment?'

'I've succeeded in making you invisible, Alfred! In-vi-si-ble! You are *invisible*, Alfred! Can you understand what a momentous achievement this is?'

'All too well, sir. All too well. Now, if sir does not mind, I would like to go back to how I was before.'

'Certainly, my dear Alfred. Certainly. Wait there, I'll fetch the bottle myself. You'll see, two spoonfuls should be ample, and then you'll be able to look yourself in the mirror again.'

A few moments later, Alfred was still invisible, though the red bottle was now empty.

'I knew it,' he lamented. 'I knew it…'

'Oh, cheer up, Alfred. Put yourself in *my* shoes: how do you think *I* feel about having an invisible servant? To see my breakfast tray carried in by a puff of air? Anyway, all is not lost. You never know, I may yet stumble on the correct formula…'

'Sir, you would be well advised to do that.'

'I beg your pardon?'

'You would be well advised to return me to my original state. Otherwise you will not know a minute's peace, I swear to you.'

'You dare to threaten me? You've lost your mind, Alfred!'

'Among other things, yes. But I intend to get them back. Otherwise, I say again, you will not know a minute's peace. Ah! Perhaps you don't believe me? Well, in that case I'd better give you a little demonstration...'

For the next few seconds, Alfred was silent. This was in spite of his master's repeated efforts to locate him, swinging his arms and moving around the room, but only grasping empty air. Exhausted, he sank into an armchair, thought for a moment, then looked about the room with an expression of menace. 'Oh, Alfred, I think I'm beginning to understand. But if you...'

He was interrupted by the doorbell, which he got up to answer himself. A pretty young woman with platinum blonde hair entered the room and threw herself into his arms.

'Harvey, my love, at long last!'

'Judith, my darling...'

The couple kissed in a passionate embrace, and then the lovely Judith studied her companion. 'Harvey dear, whatever's the matter? Don't tell me your wife is coming home early? You promised we'd have two whole days... two days of bliss...'

The telephone rang, freezing them in place.

'I'd better answer it,' declared Harvey. 'If it's Sarah and I don't answer...'

But then the ringing abruptly ceased. Judith's eyes widened and she let out a blood-curdling scream. 'Harvey! Why, it answered itself!'

Harvey stared at the telephone, then leapt forward to grab it.

'Hello, yes? Oh, Sarah! Sorry, darling? But of course I'm alone! Who else might be here? A scream? Oh, yes! What am I thinking! That was me… Yes, it was… I twisted my ankle as I was running for the telephone… I was afraid I might miss you, you see… No, it's quite all right now…'

With that, Harvey tumbled to the ground, landing on his hands and knees. Judith let out a scream even more piercing than the first, and then silence descended. The master of the house lunged for the receiver, which lay on the ground beside him.

'Hello? Sarah, are you still there? What? No, it was nothing, I assure you… Ah! The scream, yes of course… It's Alfred. He's rehearsing… Yes, he thinks he's an actor now… Shakespeare, yes… But listen, there's nothing at all for you to worry about. Everything here is perfectly fine…'

The first act of *The Invisible Man* at the Theatre Royal reached its end to thunderous applause. And so did the second act, at which point 'Harvey' took the opportunity to introduce his co-stars.

'And in the role of Judith – Nathalie Marvel!'

The blonde beauty received warm applause – almost as much as the leading man, whom she introduced in turn, 'Ladies and gentlemen, Nigel Manson.'

The show was a triumph.

Two gentlemen sitting in the centre of the stalls waited patiently for their neighbours – who were themselves impeded by slow movement along the aisles – to finally leave.

'A well-deserved success, Twist. I see now why it's been playing to sold-out crowds for two weeks. I'm glad I let you convince me to come along.'

Archibald Hurst, a burly, ruddy-faced man in his fifties, was not a regular theatregoer. His vocation as a Scotland Yard inspector left him with little time or inclination for it. He had a knack – a real knack, all his colleagues agreed – for stumbling upon the most baffling cases. Fortunately enough, his friend Dr Alan Twist was regularly on hand to advise him.

Twist was a renowned criminologist who knew just how to counsel the inspector. All the same, it had taken considerable effort to convince Hurst to accompany him to the Theatre Royal that night. Twist was tall and very thin, with a habitually placid expression and gentle eyes that gleamed from behind his *pince-nez*.

'I'm delighted, Archibald,' he said. 'I hope you'll come with me more often in future.'

'For actors of this calibre, certainly. Nigel Manson, Nathalie Marvel – both splendid. And all those scenes with the invisible man… I haven't laughed so much in years. By the way, did you know Nigel Manson wrote the play as well?'

'Yes, I heard. Though I can't help but think a certain Mr Wells might have had something to do with it. Anyway, his performance was remarkable, as was Miss Marvel's.'

'With two great comic performers like that, there were bound to be sparks onstage…'

'Sparks, yes. A very apt choice of words, my friend.'

Hurst frowned. 'What do you mean?'

Dr Alan Twist removed his *pince-nez* and began to polish the lenses with his handkerchief. Only when they were clean did he continue. 'Did you see the way they kissed?'

'The way they——? Oh, Twist, it was only pretend! But I admit it was damned convincing.'

'Too convincing, in my opinion. And don't forget the way they looked at one another.'

'Those were their characters! Young lovers are *supposed* to look at one another like that.'

Dr Twist gave a shrug. 'Anyway, there are rumours going around. Nigel Manson met Nathalie Marvel at the first rehearsal two or three months ago…'

'Well, I suppose it's good to hear that you don't *only* read the crime reports in the newspapers…'

'They say she set her sights on him from the very beginning. Now, as I'm sure you know, my dear Archibald, Nigel Manson has been married for less than a year.'

'So? I never said Manson was a saint. What does it matter? You know as well as I do the lives those people lead…'

Dr Twist's blue eyes took on a faraway expression. 'It would be a rather unusual coincidence. Not only does the beautiful Nathalie Marvel play the role of Manson's mistress onstage, but offstage too…'

'It's rather comical in a way, don't you think?' said the inspector cheerfully, before getting achily to his feet. 'He has only one thing to worry about.'

'Which is?'

'Let's hope the invisible man doesn't start bothering him offstage too.'

7

Creeping Dread

Standing beside the open window, Helen Manson gazed impassively at the Dartmoor hills, unmoved by their beauty at sunset. She could not suppress a shudder at the sight of Wish Tor, with its curious shape silhouetted darkly against the amber horizon. She jumped when she heard her husband's voice.

'Something the matter, darling?'

Something the matter? He dared to ask her that, knowing full well she was consumed by anger and jealousy?

Still standing by the window, unmoving, a tightness rising in her throat, she considered the last twelve months of their marriage. On their honeymoon last summer, there had not been a single cloud in sight. But only a few weeks later, they had begun to gather.

She was intrigued at first by Nigel's unusual enthusiasm for this new comedy he was working on. But as soon as she met his young co-star, she knew their marriage was in trouble. Nathalie Marvel, with her hair that was much too blonde, had not left a favourable impression on Helen Manson. Nor had her manager, Frank Holloway.

Naturally, Helen attended the opening night of *The Invisible Man*, and the play's immediate success briefly tempered her jealousy. But Nathalie Marvel's performance was much too provocative, in her view. And then the rumours began to circulate…

Helen did not let herself believe them, of course. Whenever

she was bothered by her husband's lengthy absences, she told herself it was simply the price of his success. Fortune had smiled on them, what was she complaining about? After all, Nigel's fame and material success continued to grow apace.

In the middle of May he informed her that he was preparing a wonderful surprise for her. When pressed, he refused to supply even the tiniest hint. This went on for two whole months, until a few days ago when he cheerfully declared, 'Pack your bags, Helen darling, we're going away for a couple of weeks!'

'Where to?'

'Ah, but that's the surprise! You remember when we drove across Dartmoor, and spotted that old house…'

'The one with the terrible history? The one that gave you the idea for *The Invisible Man*?'

'That's the one. It was for sale, do you remember? Well, I bought it! For next to nothing, actually. The restoration work over the last couple of months has cost a bit more than expected, but no matter! I've developed a real fondness for the place, it will make an excellent country retreat!'

'And that's where you're taking me?' said Helen.

'Why, yes. We leave tomorrow morning, and I guarantee you won't be disappointed. I'm told they've worked miracles on the landscaping. And as for the house itself, they've renovated it entirely – all except for the east wing, which has been preserved as it was. It has an atmosphere I couldn't bear to see ruined by modernisation. Oh! Before I forget, Frank and Nathalie will be joining us for the weekend as well.'

Helen scarcely slept a wink that night. It was difficult to say which prospect was more dreadful: spending the night in that sinister manor, or putting up with that impudent creature taunting her – even if only for a weekend. And then there was Nigel, who slept peacefully in the twin bed beside hers. She would gladly have shaken him awake.

She knew there was no way out of it; she would simply have to brave the onslaught with as serene an outlook as possible.

Therefore, when the manor came into view some twenty-four hours later, she greeted it with a smile. Its facade was no less forbidding, but she had to concede that its surroundings were considerably more pleasant – particularly considering the tangle of untamed foliage which had held sway there the previous year. A splendid magnolia tree stood in the centre of the lawn, while the rest of the grounds were garlanded with colourful flowerbeds and late-blooming rhododendron bushes. The whole display was penned in by a belt of ancient trees.

Nigel took her by the hand and escorted her around the house, pointing out the various improvements with undisguised pride.

'The walls are virtually untouched, as you can see. Except for the paint on the doorframes, of course. The bedrooms are in the west wing. The drawing room is upstairs. Right this way…'

He led her to the aforesaid drawing room, explaining that he had chosen this room because it offered the most beautiful view of the moor. Which it undeniably did, Helen thought, as she stood by the large window overlooking the driveway.

By the time her husband had finished showing her the west wing, Helen had overcome her negative first impression. There was nothing sinister about the house, and the interior modernisation was rather successful. The couple dined on a cold collation served by Jenny, the cook's daughter – those two were the sum total of the domestic staff.

It wasn't until after the meal that Nigel showed her the untouched east wing, with the staircase where the long-ago tragedy had taken place. She was seized by a distinct feeling of unease, as though the faded tapestries themselves were steeped in menace. She followed Nigel without a word as he led her up the old oaken staircase, each step groaning underfoot. On the upper landing – lit only by the candlestick in Nigel's hand – her feeling of disquiet worsened, as though an evil force slumbered nearby. Right on the spot where she stood, a woman had been thrown down the stairs, though neither human nor animal had stood anywhere near her.

A door slammed, making Helen jump.

'Poor Helen,' Nigel mocked. 'There's nothing to be frightened of, it was only a draught!'

That night, she did not sleep well.

The next day, Friday, there was nothing particular that disturbed her, but the fact of Nathalie's imminent arrival was sufficient to ruin her mood. And then came Saturday, bringing with it Nigel's two unwelcome guests.

It was only five hours since Nathalie Marvel and Frank Holloway's arrival. A five-hour nightmare, during which Helen had endured Nathalie's false cheer, her unconvincing smiles, her affected sympathy. Then there was the ironic gleam in Frank Holloway's eyes as he watched Nigel rushing back and forth to ensure his guests had everything they wanted. Of course, he wasn't fooled by the display. Nor was Helen – she found it deeply humiliating.

At the moment, Frank and Nathalie were settling into their respective rooms. It was a fifteen minute lull, which could have lasted all night for all Helen cared. She was on edge, and waited a moment or two before answering her husband, who had the nerve – the absolute *temerity* – to ask if there was something the matter.

'Something the matter? What could be the matter, for God's sake?'

She was dying to tell him she couldn't bear to spend five more minutes in the company of that brazen, brainless woman, and that she would not be held responsible for her actions if she did. But, with a great effort, she refrained from doing so.

She remembered only too well how Nigel had reacted when, in a moment of recklessness, she had told him what she really thought of the young actress, and of the extracurricular activities in which the two of them indulged. All it took was a single mention of the word 'divorce' from Nigel to silence her. That sort of drastic action went against her nature, and besides, she did still love her husband in spite of everything. Whenever he'd tried to bring up the subject subsequently, she'd avoided the question. She nurtured a small hope that sooner or later he would realise the ridiculousness of his behaviour; that he would see the girl for what she truly was: a pretty face, an impossible shade of blonde hair, and very little else.

She turned towards Nigel, who sat in an armchair leafing distractedly through a film magazine.

'By the way,' he said, 'have I told you about the contract I signed for the US tour?'

'US tour?' Helen stammered. 'When? For how long?'

Nigel ran a hand carelessly through his hair. 'Before the end of the year. As for how long, that will depend on how successful it turns out to be. But barring any unforeseen events, it should be a few months.'

Helen felt as though her throat were caught in a vice. 'A few months? And... she'll be there, too?'

'Who?'

'Nathalie, that's who. Don't play innocent.'

'Of course. Without *her*, there's no "Invisible Man". As I'm sure you know.'

A silence hung between them, heavy with unspoken words. To cut it short, and to preserve the mood of artificial good cheer, Nigel changed the subject. 'By the way, are you coming out with us this evening? Frank and I are planning to go to the pub in the village. I dropped in yesterday and met a few local characters. A rather stuffy philosophy professor, a drunkard, and one of those very friendly country doctors. Quite a trio. We shan't be bored in their company, I can tell you that much!'

'Not today. I don't feel like it. I'll probably just go to bed early. I need to catch up on my sleep.'

'Very well. You can keep Nathalie company. She'll be staying behind too.'

8

The Star-Maker

Arap on the door, and Frank Holloway entered the bedroom.

Nathalie Marvel wrapped a canary-yellow robe around herself and turned to him. 'Frank! It's you! You could at least—'

'Knock? But I did, my dear,' he said with a luminous smile. He went over to the window seat, made himself comfortable, and lit a cigarette. He studied the young actress through the smoke.

Frank Holloway was an unusual man – perpetually smiling, even when he was insulted. At least, that's what people who did not know him well tended to think. In reality, his mood was always discernible in his eyes. Their blue irises darkened in anger or brightened in good cheer. He had a roguish air about him; one theatre critic called him a 'loveable rogue' – which was a fairly accurate description. He was of average height, still slim now that he was in his forties, and wore smart, sober suits. The roguishness lay in his vast selection of ties – all natural silk, of course. But he always wore the same pearl-studded tie pin, a distinctive pair of gold signet rings, and, to complete the ensemble, a splendid Panama hat, which was very becoming to his olive complexion and silvery temples. During the winter months, this was replaced by a wide-brimmed fedora, and the ties gave way to cravats. This gave him a certain continental air, which proved a hit with the ladies.

Nathalie Marvel, for one, had found it impossible to resist.

Though beautiful and effortlessly graceful, it was the actress's long, fluttering black eyelashes which gave her the charming, ingenuous aura that so delighted the press. But it did not come easily; indeed this trick required many hours of work in front of her mirror. It seemed like only yesterday that Frank first saw her practising in a shabby hotel room, back in the days when she was merely his mistress. He had thought himself very clever when he quoted a line from *Tartuffe* – 'Cover this breast that I cannot see' – as he undressed her.

He shook his head with a feeling of nostalgia. It was not so long ago, after all.

Curiously enough, Nathalie's thoughts followed a similar path, albeit with less affection. She too remembered the line he had quoted, and chided herself for giggling like an idiot at the time. It was only three years ago, but it seemed much longer. She was not even twenty then.

They had roamed up and down England on a never-ending tour of rundown theatres. It was a lean period, but not all that much worse than the life she had known before; the perilous acrobatics that barely paid enough to survive. Yes, she had been forced to grit her teeth on more than one occasion during those years, biting back the despair in pursuit of a dream which she truly believed Frank Holloway could provide. He was adept at making promises to young women who were eager to appear on stage.

She could still remember the evening they first dined together, when he had lavished her with flattery about her promise as an actress and informed her that lasting success was a positive guarantee. That magnetic smile, the gold signet rings shimmering under her admiring eyes, and the wine glass he refilled after nearly every sip.

It did not take long for her to realise the truth. Frank was strictly small-time, and more interested in his clients' bodies than their performances onstage. It was a bitter realisation, which had left her deeply depressed. Strangely enough, it was only then that Frank seemed to start taking her career seriously.

He pushed her to work tirelessly, and invested a great deal of his own money in shows where she topped the bill. And then her luck finally began to turn. Once her dream started coming true, it was perhaps the swiftest turnaround a young actress could have hoped for.

Frank was also reliving the recent past, and still staring stubbornly at Nathalie. He had sensed from the beginning that Nigel Manson's play would be a hit. He had also known from the moment he introduced the actor to Nathalie that he would soon lose his mistress. He had rarely seen eyes as fiery with lust as Nathalie's were that day. Forty-eight hours later, she announced coldly that from now on their relationship would be purely professional. Within a week, she was begging him to keep their former affair a secret.

'Tell me, Nat,' he said, stroking his chin, 'why don't you want Nigel to know that you and I——?'

'Well,' she replied, studying herself in the mirror, 'I think it would create an atmosphere that might prove detrimental to our work.'

'May I remind you that you didn't hesitate to seduce a married man? So I doubt you're in any position to talk about peaceful working conditions…'

'All right, if you want the truth, here it is: I'm sure if he found out that I'd had an affair with *you*, he would be disgusted.'

'Well, at least that's honest. But it's not very kind, Nat. You seem to have rather a short memory.'

'What do you mean?'

'You seem to have forgotten everything I've done for you.'

Nathalie turned sharply towards him, as though stung by a wasp. 'Is that a joke, Frank? Do you seriously believe that if I were ungrateful I would have signed the paper you put in front of me last week? I didn't *have* to give you a penny of the proceeds from the American tour.'

'Come on, Nat. I'm not talking about money.'

'What, then?'

'Well… All I'm saying is that if you ever got lonely, you know that your old friend will always be here.'

She eyed him sternly, shrugged, then turned back to her dressing table. Leaning forward, she knocked a bottle of perfume onto the marble floor.

'All right, all right. Don't be angry, Nat. That's all I'm saying. But tell me, what's the matter? You're not yourself just now, are you? I don't think I've ever seen you as nervous as you were on the journey today. And as for all your smiles at Nigel's wife, I wasn't fooled for a moment. I know you enjoy being polite to her because it drives her mad, but I think you went a bit overboard.'

The actress's eyes welled up with tears, which she immediately wiped away in an angry sweep of her hand.

'Watch the mascara, Nat…'

'Leave me alone!'

'Problems with Nigel?' Frank ventured. 'What's the situation, exactly? Are you still planning to get married?'

'He wants to, but he needs a divorce first.'

'And what about you? Are you still interested?'

'Yes, but…'

'But?' repeated Frank with a flicker of interest between his narrowed eyelids.

'Well, I don't know what's the matter with him lately… Renovating this old hovel in the middle of nowhere, for one thing, and without saying a word to me!'

'He wanted to surprise you…'

'Surprise me?' Nathalie snapped, her eyes flashing with anger. 'It was a surprise, all right! He told me at the beginning of the month that he wanted me to spend a weekend in the country with him…'

'Well, he couldn't have invited you all by yourself, could he? What would his wife think?'

'That's not the point. He stubbornly refused to tell me where we were going, and only let us know the address forty-eight hours before we set out!'

'But Nathalie, surely that's what he meant by *surprise*! I don't understand…'

'You think it's as simple as that, do you? What possessed him to buy this old shack in such a remote part of the world? Can you explain *that*?'

'But I just told you… Nat, come on, don't get upset. It's ridiculous. I knew we shouldn't have made the trip all in one go, you're obviously exhausted.'

'Yes… yes, I suppose so,' she said, taking her head in her hands.

Frank Holloway got to his feet and then sighed. 'I take it you're not coming to the pub with us tonight?'

'Spend an evening with a bunch of boring old men? I don't think so, do you?'

9

Murder

THE NEXT DAY, SUNDAY, WAS A GLORIOUS one. The windows of Trerice Manor sparkled in the sunlight, and the air carried the musical chirp of birdsong. The smile on Nigel Manson's face might have suggested he was in thrall to the place and its charms, but a keener eye would have noted the unease he was trying to conceal. He was still suffering the ill effects of last night's adventure at the inn, which he had not left until closing time. He also wished he were anywhere other than that drawing room at the present moment. Now, he was trapped with two people whose company he usually enjoyed – but always individually, not with each other.

The atmosphere was charged, and Nathalie's feigned nonchalance did little to improve matters. Nibbling on an arm of her sunglasses, she seemed absorbed in contemplating the two cameras which stood on the sideboard. She stared closely at their lenses, until finally turning to Helen: 'I hope you slept better than I did last night. I'd finally drifted off when Nigel came bursting into my room, stinking of beer. He told me he'd come to the wrong door…'

Helen, who toyed nervously with a small statuette on the mantelpiece, did not say a word.

Apparently untroubled by her hostess's disdain, Nathalie wandered over to the window humming 'Tea for Two' and glanced outside.

'It's a nice day, Nigel. Would you mind lending me one of your cameras? I'd like to take some pictures in the garden.'

'Certainly,' said the actor, 'we've got the weather for it, all right. But don't take too long. We're expecting visitors, you know.'

'Gentlemen from the village,' Helen interjected with an unnaturally bright smile, 'who would be so disappointed not to see the sublime Miss Nathalie Marvel in the flesh.'

A brief look of confusion flickered across Nathalie's face, but she instantly recovered, and returned Helen's smile. 'Oh, don't worry. I shan't go far. And I'll be back very soon.'

With that, she replaced her sunglasses on the bridge of her piquant nose and left the room, grabbing a camera as she went.

The couple stood in silence for a long time, before Helen went over to the coffee table where refreshments had been laid out. She poured herself a glass of tonic water and said, 'By the way, who exactly are these guests of ours?'

'I told you before, I don't remember exactly. We were utterly sloshed, Frank and I...'

'But *he* wasn't the one handing out invitations, was he?'

'True. But let's not exaggerate – I asked two or three people to stop by for a drink after lunch, that's all.' He rubbed his forehead. 'Let's see... there was a philosophy teacher, I think – what was his name...? Sitwell, that was it! Then there's a Dr Grant, and a very colourful local character...'

'Well, it's nearly three o'clock and nobody's here. Are you quite sure of what you're saying?'

'Of course I'm sure. Besides, Frank mentioned it at lunch as well. Where has he got to, I wonder?'

'What *I'm* wondering is how you managed to mistake our bedroom door for Miss Marvel's last night. They aren't in the same part of the house. They're not even on the same floor.'

'Hey, I can see somebody coming up the drive,' said Nigel,

having drifted over to the large window. 'You see? I can't have been as drunk as I thought.'

Within five minutes, Dr Thomas Grant was seated in an armchair and chatting with his hosts in a low, toneless voice. 'At my age, I really have no excuse for such debauchery. To think I spend my days preaching moderation in all its forms to my patients, and then I go and do something like that… Victor always says "the important thing in life is to be consistent in your behaviour," and I quite agree with him.'

'I'd be surprised if you were in as sorry a state as Nigel,' Helen declared cheerfully, grinning at her husband, who stood by the window stealing occasional glances out at the garden. 'He barely remembers inviting anybody over at all!'

'*I* don't remember it in the slightest,' replied the old GP, 'it was Victor who dropped by to remind me just before noon. To my shame, I had only just woken up.'

'Come now, Doctor, don't be so hard on yourself,' protested Nigel over his shoulder. 'Victor? Do you mean your friend Professor Victor Sitwell?'

'Yes… he shouldn't be too long now,' said Dr Grant, glancing at the clock, 'it's almost three-fifteen.'

Helen got up from the sofa and approached her husband, but she paused by the fireplace when she saw him wave to someone beyond the wide-open window. 'Hey, Nat!' he called out. 'Are you coming to join us?'

The young actress had just come across the lawn and now paused on the driveway below. She looked up at Nigel's smiling face fifty feet above her. 'Yes, I'll be right there,' she said. 'But first, let me take your picture.'

'Certainly,' declared the actor, puffing out his chest and placing his hand triumphantly on his hips. 'Wait a moment, I have an idea.'

In a single bound, he was up on the window sill. He settled

there, swinging his legs over the edge, arms folded, leaning against the window frame with an easygoing grin.

Although quite used to seeing her husband perform these feats of acrobatics in pursuit of a photograph, Helen seemed disconcerted – even embarrassed. She turned away, and began toying with the statuette on the mantelpiece once more.

'There!' cried Nigel. 'Now, snap away!'

Nathalie nodded, peering up in admiration. Then she raised the camera and framed her co-star in the viewfinder. She pressed the shutter once.

There would be no second photograph.

10

An Inspector Calls

With a sigh of regret and mild annoyance, Dr Alan Twist went out to answer the doorbell. He'd been enjoying a peaceful evening in his London apartment, and was now torn from his reading – an insightful study of several unsolved murders dating back to the last century. The first thing he noticed about his visitor was an unruly forelock – indeed, it was always the first thing he noticed when meeting his friend Inspector Archibald Hurst. Hurst's thinning hair was usually neatly combed; anything else was an ill omen – a barometer for the Scotland Yard man's mood.

This time, though, he did not seem to be in low spirits. Twist sensed a mild hint of irritation and perplexity, that was all. But it was not until Hurst was settled and had, of course, indulged in the usual pleasantries about the weather and his friend's health, that he explained the reason for his visit.

'By the way, do you recall when you took me to the theatre to see that Nigel Manson play, *The Invisible Man*?'

'Certainly. It was a rare pleasure, my dear fellow.'

'Well, you know I'm a busy man. Unlike you, of course! I'll wager you've spent your day with your nose buried in some criminology tome.'

'Right you are, but how did you know that?'

Hurst gave a shrug intended to convey modesty, though it was belied by his somewhat smug grin. 'Simple deduction. Only criminology books keep you from reading the newspapers.'

'And what makes you so sure I haven't been reading the newspapers?'

'I doubt you would have missed a piece about Nigel Manson's death, would you?'

Stunned, Twist removed his pince-nez.

'Let me remind you,' the policeman continued, 'that when the show was over I made a playful remark that I hoped the "invisible man" wouldn't bother him offstage as well as on. Do you recall that? Well, that seems to be exactly what happened two days ago in a small village on Dartmoor. Nigel Manson fell from the upstairs window of his house – pushed by an invisible man. He was killed instantly.'

Twist stared at his friend for a moment. 'Pushed… by an invisible man?'

'That's what the witnesses said.'

'And these witnesses claim to have seen an invisible man?'

'Yes. Or rather, *not* seen him.'

'Perhaps you'd better tell me from the beginning.'

Hurst removed a notebook from his pocket, settled back in his armchair, and began. 'The details I'm about to share with you have not yet been released to the press. They've reported Manson's death as a simple accident, and it's quite possible the coroner's jury will agree with them. But here are the facts.

'The incident took place at an old house which Nigel Manson had recently finished renovating. He was spending a few days there on holiday with his wife. It was exactly 3:15 p.m. last Sunday when he stepped up onto the window sill so that Nathalie Marvel could take a picture of him. She was there for the weekend with her manager, Frank Holloway.

'Nathalie was outside the house, on the driveway below, looking up at the drawing room window where Manson was posing. Apart from Manson himself, there were two other people in the room with him – his wife Helen, and Dr Thomas Grant, the village physician – and Frank Holloway was just stepping through the doorway. The fifth and final witness was another new friend of Manson's, one Professor Victor Sitwell. He was walking up the driveway towards the house at the fateful moment.

'Sitwell had already caught a glimpse of Manson on the window sill as he approached the front gate; he didn't realise right away that the fellow was having his picture taken. But he clearly recognised the look of horror and surprise on Manson's face in the second before he fell. Not to mention the way he flailed with his hands, trying to save himself. He claims there was no one standing behind Manson when he fell. Nathalie was taking a photograph at that moment, so she had a front-row seat, you might say. But since she was directly below the window, she couldn't see whether or not there was anyone standing behind him. But she *is* quite certain he was pushed by… "something". He was smiling quite happily down at her, when suddenly he came toppling forward. She describes it the same as Sitwell: a look of sudden terror, and the hands reaching out to try to save himself. He landed right in front of her. Well, a few feet away, anyway – dead on the paving stones.

'In the drawing room, Dr Thomas Grant was sitting in an armchair angled slightly away from the window. The actor was on the periphery of his vision, but he would, of course, have seen if "something" had pushed him. Frank Holloway was coming through the door just as Manson fell, and he's positive that there was no one anywhere near him.

'But the most convincing testimony comes from Helen Manson. She was by the fireplace, roughly nine or ten feet from her husband, and saw the whole thing clearly. He was perfectly still, striking a pose, when suddenly he was shoved in the back and fell forward, into the void. She's quite certain he didn't lose his balance. It was too sudden for that. And she's absolutely positive no one was standing anywhere near him. The only thing she noticed was a slight draught in the seconds before he fell.'

The inspector closed his notebook. 'Well, what do you make of it?'

Dr Twist had closed his eyes while Hurst was speaking, and now opened them again. He remained silent and thoughtful for a few moments before replying, 'It sounds like one of those delightfully sinister ghost stories we are so fond of in that part of England. It seems as if there is hardly a square foot of Dartmoor without some dreadful tale of the supernatural attached to it. As for this particular tale, I cannot comment. I'd need to study the scene, to meet and listen to the accounts of each witness, before I ventured a theory. But the idea of an accident – or at least, an accidental fall – seems to be ruled out by the testimonies you've recorded. The same goes for suicide. At least, that would be very unusual behaviour for someone actively trying to end their own life. Which leaves murder. Of course, that's downright impossible. And yet, it seems to be the explanation you find the most appealing… The victim was in a play about an invisible man, and his wife noticed a draught before he went tumbling out of the window. Rather weak, don't you think?'

'Actually… it's not exactly *my* explanation,' said the inspector, looking a little embarrassed. 'It's the Superintendent's. He came into my office this morning to tell me that an old friend of his, the Chief Constable over in Tavistock, has a very unusual murder on his hands, which might require the advice of a specialist…'

Hurst cleared his throat, evidently still flush with pride at the Superintendent's compliment. '*I* thought,' he continued quickly, 'the whole thing sounded rather strange. My conclusion was similar to yours, but he wouldn't hear of it. Anyway, I agreed to take the case. So, the next step is to hear what each witness has to say in person before forming an opinion. I reckon that's the key to solving this mess. These country policemen aren't experienced enough to deal with this sort of thing, where you have to tease the truth out of people. But I'm pretty confident.'

There was a glimmer of mischief behind Dr Twist's *pince-nez*. 'So I gather. But pride comes before a fall, you know. This case is decidedly peculiar. Just because the murder hypothesis seems to be the least likely, doesn't mean it should be dismissed outright. In fact, I'd call it "improbable" rather than "impossible". Because if we forget the physical circumstances for a moment, the rumours circulating about Nathalie Marvel and Nigel Manson seem rather well-founded. Husband, wife and mistress, all under one roof? Sounds like a lethal cocktail to me! And then it turns out that both wife and mistress are key witnesses to this curious defenestration, which everybody agrees was no accident. Add to that the Superintendent's rather curious behaviour – he must have had a reason for presenting the case to you as he did…'

Hurst nodded sagely, then said, 'In my opinion, if it's murder then it must be someone from Nigel Manson's immediate circle. That is, his wife, Nathalie Marvel or Frank Holloway. Let's not dwell on *how* the crime was committed. You saw the play, just as I did: the servant's transformation into "invisible man" was spectacular; the killer must have appropriated one of those theatrical effects. And neither of the women lacks motive: jealousy, revenge, not to mention the question of Manson's money. The impresario is admittedly more difficult to pin down, but you know as well as I do that personal *and* business relationships in the theatrical world are often more complex than they appear.'

'If my experience has taught me anything, it's that *everything* is more complex than it appears. Now answer me this, Archibald: when do we leave?'

'Well… early tomorrow morning. I've booked a couple of rooms at the Red Lion, a pub near the house. But…' Hurst's mouth dropped open. '"We"?' he repeated. 'Does that mean you'll...?'

'Come now, Archibald, you didn't doubt it for a second, did you? Obviously you came here to ask me to accompany you. And you knew I wouldn't refuse. To tell you the truth, my friend, I think a little trip to Dartmoor might be just what the doctor ordered.'

11

The Investigation

THE FOLLOWING EVENING, DR TWIST AND INSPECTOR Hurst stood before the grand façade of Trerice Manor. Of all the large windows glowing in the reflected rays of waning sunlight, it was, of course, the drawing room window that was the object of their attention, and the large granite paving stones below it.

'And that's where he hit the ground,' declared the unimpressive little man who accompanied them. Colonel Weston looked like many things, but a Chief Constable was not one of them. Hurst, like many others before him, had been wrong-footed by his first impression, and imperiously instructed him to notify his superiors that the men from Scotland Yard had arrived. Although Weston had a sense of humour, and bore no grudges, the misunderstanding had shaken Hurst's confidence.

'He landed on his right parietal bone,' Weston continued. 'Killed instantly, of course. Miss Marvel was standing where we are now. And Professor Sitwell also witnessed the fall. He was over there…' The Chief Constable turned back and pointed to an area somewhere beyond the rhododendron bushes, about thirty yards across the lawn. 'And of course he came running over. He was joined about a minute later by Basil Hawkins, whom I've already told you about – another of the invited guests. It was the sound of the two women screaming that brought him over, because he hadn't seen the fall. He must have missed it by seconds, though, since he was hot on Sitwell's heels all the way from the village.

'And upstairs in the drawing room were Manson's wife, Dr Grant and Mr Holloway. They… Well, perhaps it would be best for you to interview them yourselves.'

Hurst nodded, his eyes still fixed on the façade. 'Have you had the window examined? And those either side of it? What about the frame, and the roof directly above?'

Weston smiled. 'There's nothing to stop you from carrying out your own examination, but I assure you it would be a waste of time. We've been through the whole place with a fine-tooth comb. That includes the drawing room up there, and the paving stones down here. Nothing. Not a thing. Not a clue – not even the tiniest scratch. Just the body, and the camera smashed into a thousand pieces. The girl dropped it in shock.'

'Hold on a moment,' said Hurst, struck by a thought. 'Have you tried—?'

'The roll of film? Yes, we checked it,' interrupted Weston. 'Fortunately it survived the fall, and wasn't exposed to the light, so we had it developed. Unfortunately, though, it's of no use to us.'

'So, Miss Marvel took a picture of Nigel Manson before he fell?' Hurst exclaimed.

'She did. But it tells us nothing, I can assure you of that. We've practically worn it out with endless examinations. I know that in mystery novels that kind of "evidence" usually contains a vital clue, but there's nothing there. I'll show it to you if you really want to see it…'

'I do, very much,' said Hurst, his round face breaking into a sly smile as wide as the gulf he perceived between the observational skills of the provincial police and those of Scotland Yard. 'By the way, Colonel, you haven't told us your own personal theory yet?'

Weston seemed visibly embarrassed by the question, and cleared his throat before answering. 'Perhaps you'd better interview the witnesses first, so as not to cloud your judgement.'

'He didn't slip or lose his balance, I know that much. I had him framed in the centre of the viewfinder, and was just about to snap a second picture. He was sitting on the window sill, smiling down at me when it happened. All of a sudden, he was thrown forward, as though someone had pushed him from behind.'

There was only one feature of Nathalie Marvel's personality that her prodigious acting talent could not conceal: the chilly determination in her eyes, a reflection of the innate stubbornness that had ultimately brought her professional success. She did her best to hide it behind those fluttering eyelashes of hers as she spoke to the detectives who had knocked on her bedroom door some five minutes earlier. It was also masked by the sunglasses she had slipped onto her adorable little nose to hide those beautiful grey eyes, now pink and puffy from weeping.

Were they real tears? Dr Twist could not have sworn to it. She was probably more troubled by the loss of her co-star than that of her lover.

'And you didn't see anyone standing behind him?' asked Hurst.

'No... but I didn't have the best view from where I was standing.'

'Not even a shadow?'

Nathalie Marvel hesitated. 'No, I don't think so... But then again, I was directly below, so it was difficult for me to...'

'What about anywhere else? In one of the other windows, for instance, or up on the roof?'

The actress thought about this carefully for a moment, then affirmed, 'No, I'm absolutely certain. From where I was positioned I definitely would have spotted that.'

The Scotland Yard inspector nodded and made a note of this on his little pad. 'And,' he said, 'what happened then?'

'I don't remember. I screamed, the camera fell from my hands… a man came running up behind me… there was screaming from the window upstairs, too… and then another man came running, some sort of vagrant, I think. After that, I don't recall. Somebody escorted me up the stairs, then gave me something to drink…' She sniffed, took out her handkerchief and dabbed at her eyes beneath the sunglasses.

'All right, that'll do for the moment. Now I'd like to ask you about something that's perhaps less painful, but just as delicate, Miss Marvel. Can you think of anybody who may have had a grudge against Nigel Manson?'

The actress whipped off her sunglasses and answered without hesitation. 'Yes. One person, and one person only. She's the only one – to my knowledge – who had any reason to murder him. But apparently, she couldn't have done it.'

'Presumably you're referring to Mrs Manson?' said Dr Twist, peering at her over his *pince-nez*.

The actress's eyes retained their defiant gleam. 'She inherits his money, doesn't she? And she's as jealous as a tiger.'

'You were rivals, then?'

'Not much point trying to hide it, is there? She was dying of envy. Desperate not to show it, but believe me, it showed! She could hardly contain herself when Frank and I got here on Saturday…'

Dr Twist asked her to recount the incident, which she did, painting a deeply unflattering portrait of Helen Manson into the bargain.

'Very good,' said Twist when she had finished. 'Now, let's move on. Your manager and Nigel Manson went for a little walk to the inn, leaving the two of you here alone…'

'Yes, but in our own rooms, of course.'

'And the gentlemen returned at roughly two o'clock in the morning, quite drunk…?'

'That's right. Nigel…' She bit her lip.

'Go on,' said Twist, feigning detachment. Really, he was admiring the fleeting expression of uncertainty on the young woman's face, which seemed so much more natural and becoming than the hardened veneer of the tough, professional actress.

Obviously, she felt as though she had let something slip. With a shrug, she replied, 'Well, Nigel came into my room. But it's not what you think – he just came to the wrong door. He was completely drunk, you understand. I told him to leave immediately, and he did. But that's not the point. Unfortunately, I happened to mention the incident the next day and Mrs Manson… went very pale. After that, I went outside.'

'Is it fair to assume that your sudden desire to photograph the garden was really just an excuse?'

'Naturally. There was a horrid atmosphere in that room, so I decided to beat a hasty retreat. She must have been stewing over what I'd just said and… now that I think about it… if only I hadn't asked Nigel to pose in the window…'

'But didn't he sit on the window sill of his own accord?'

'Yes, of course.'

'And you told us earlier,' Twist persisted, 'that it wouldn't have been possible for Mrs Manson to push her husband out of the window.'

'Yes. At least, that's my understanding.'

'So this is where our inquiry falters,' Hurst interjected. 'Your testimony – like everybody else's – categorically refutes both the accident theory and the suicide theory. That leaves murder, and only an invisible man could have done it. Which reminds me, incidentally, Twist and I had the pleasure of seeing a performance of your play recently. You were remarkable. But what really interests me at the moment – you can probably imagine what I am about to say – is the way the servant was able to disappear and reappear. What's the trick?'

'Well, it's a trapdoor in the stage, operated by a stagehand. The smokescreen and the lighting prevent the audience from noticing, that's all.'

'Simple, yet remarkably well executed,' commented Dr Twist. 'And there's nothing else to it?'

'No.'

Hurst shook his head in weary annoyance. 'A trapdoor and a stagehand – that's no help at all. Obviously the murderer – if there is one – couldn't have used that method. A pity; I was rather counting on that.' He had begun nervously drumming the arms of his chair. 'You see, Miss, what bothers me greatly about this story is the strange similarity between your private life and the play you performed onstage. I'm sure you've noticed the coincidence. In the play, you and your lover are tormented by an invisible man. And in reality, all the evidence suggests Mr Manson was "bothered" by an invisible man hurling him to his death. To be perfectly honest, it feels like too much of a coincidence. Incidentally, what's going to happen now with the play? Have you discussed it with your manager yet?'

Nathalie shook her head, then told them about the proposed US tour, which they had hoped would be a roaring success.

'In short,' the inspector concluded, 'apart from Mrs Manson, who inherits her husband's estate, it seems as though his death will prove very costly for a lot of people. I doubt your manager is particularly pleased at the moment? By the way, did he and Nigel get on?'

'I doubt they would have gone out drinking together if they didn't.'

'Please answer me frankly. Were there any disagreements between them? Did Mr Holloway have any possible reason to hold a grudge against Mr Manson?'

'Frank? That's absurd. You wouldn't ask that kind of question if you knew Frank. He never holds a grudge against anyone.'

Hurst got to his feet. 'Well, in that case I think we'd better get to know him. His room is at the other end of the corridor, is that right?'

'That's right. By the way, Inspector, how long are you going to keep us all prisoner here?'

'You are quite welcome to go outside for exercise.'

'No, thanks. All things considered, I'd rather stay indoors than risk bumping into any nosy neighbours from the village. Not to mention peeping toms.'

'Ah, the price of fame,' said Hurst with a bow. 'In the meantime, I'd be very grateful if you could stay here for another day or two. That will give us a chance to find the key to this riddle.'

12

The First Complication

AFTER ONLY FIVE MINUTES IN FRANK HOLLOWAY'S company, Hurst had already formed an intractable opinion of the man: he was a crafty, phlegmatic sort, shrewd as a monkey and elusive as an eel. He plumed cigar smoke into his visitors' faces, and Hurst felt an urge to grab him by the lapels of his pearl-grey jacket and shake the self-importance out of him.

'I've known some pretty wild nights in my time, but I won't forget last Saturday any time soon,' he said, with an emphatic nod. 'In fact, I'd go so far as to say the village drunk was the most lucid of the whole bunch… at least he could still hold a tune! The doctor was completely plastered, Nigel was in a very bad way, and so was the good professor. As for me, I completely blacked out after a while. I can remember the professor telling us that a photograph on the wall belonged to him, and the innkeeper telling him he was mistaken…'

'We're not interested in the details of the evening,' said the inspector, scarcely concealing his irritation. 'We're interested in what happened after that.'

'Well, it's pretty vague. I can't recall when we left the pub, or when we got back to the house. But I *do* remember stumbling around in the dark, then finding my way upstairs, and stopping off outside Nathalie's room. The door was ajar, and there was a light on inside. She was talking to Nigel…'

'Had he ended up in the wrong room, do you think? Apparently that's what he told Miss Marvel.'

'Well... even in his state, I'd be surprised if he went to her room by accident. His room was on the ground floor. He must have gone upstairs on purpose. And it would have been a very poor show if Helen had caught them at that hour, so I decided to act as lookout, just in case. They were talking in low voices, I couldn't hear exactly what they said, but it was only talk, that's all. I think Nathalie saw me, so I scurried off to my room and went to bed. The next thing I remember is waking up a few hours later with a godawful hangover. That was at noon. The atmosphere

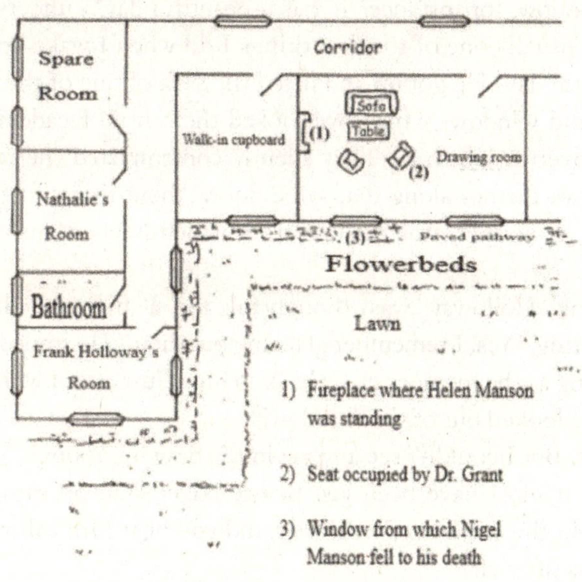

FLOORPLAN: TRERICE MANOR

(First floor, west wing)

was rather frosty – Nigel and I were feeling sorry for ourselves, but Nathalie and Helen weren't exactly full of beans either. And Nigel suddenly remembered he'd invited our drinking chums over for the afternoon, even though he couldn't really recall who they were or what time they were arriving. Which was rather annoying, I must say. He asked me if *I* could remember the plans, but as you can imagine, I wasn't much use. After lunch, I came back here to lie down for a little while. In fact, I'd only woken up a few minutes before the tragedy. I went into the drawing room, and that was the very second Nigel fell…'

'One moment,' interrupted Dr Twist. 'You said a few minutes. What exactly did you do during that time? Did you look out of the window, for instance? It was a beautiful day, I understand. That's usually one of the first things I do when I wake up on a beautiful day.' He got up and lifted the sash of one of the three bedroom windows which overlooked the central façade. Hurst went over to join him. They silently contemplated the row of windows further along that same floor. About thirty feet away (as the crow flies) was the one from which Nigel Manson had fallen.

Frank Holloway was thoughtful for a moment, before answering, 'Yes, I remember glancing out there.' He smiled now, nodding as the memory came back to him. 'Just after I woke up.'

'You looked out of this window?'

'Yes. But I couldn't see anyone in the drawing room.'

'So, it must have been just before Nigel Manson came and stood in the window. By the way, did you hear him calling out to Miss Marvel?'

The impresario raised a hand to his forehead. 'I believe I did… at some point. But only very faintly, since my windows were all closed. And of course I'd only just woken up, so I was still pretty drowsy. I put on a fresh shirt, combed my hair… and that's about it.'

'All right,' said Hurst, turning back to him. 'Let's go back over the moment you stepped into the drawing room. Tell us exactly what you saw.'

'Well… I opened the door – the one diagonally opposite the window where Nigel was sitting. I spotted him immediately, of course – it's not every day you see someone in that position. But then, only a second or two later, he… how shall I put it? He fell, and it was as if he'd been pushed violently from behind. But, of course, there was no one there.'

'And where were the other people in the room?'

'Dr Grant was in an armchair roughly equidistant between myself and Nigel. Helen was by the fireplace.'

'Were they in your eye line the entire time, or is that just what you noticed *after* Nigel fell?'

Frank Holloway looked a little uneasy. 'It's difficult to say. I don't think I saw Dr Grant right away. But I definitely caught a glimpse of Helen's silhouette. In any case, I really don't see what difference it makes? I saw them both within seconds of each other…'

Hurst narrowed his eyes and fixed the theatrical agent with a steady glare. 'So, at the moment Nigel Manson fell from the window, you weren't looking directly at the other two people in the room. Therefore, if one of them happened to move at the same time – discreetly – you wouldn't have noticed?'

A look of annoyance crossed Holloway's face, and he answered reluctantly, 'Well… it's not impossible, I suppose…'

Hurst made a few notes, then asked the witness to tell them about the actor and his co-star – specifically, the nature of their relationship. Holloway wasted no time. After explaining how he first met Nathalie, and how he had helped her along the path to fame (omitting the fact that they were lovers throughout), he finally reached the heart of the matter: Nathalie's first meeting with Nigel Manson.

'I'll never forget the look on her face when she first saw him. She was chattering away nervously the whole time, and her eyes were sparkling… I knew her well enough by then to work out what was going on. And in less than a fortnight they were "partners" in every sense of the word.'

He pulled no punches when it came to describing their plans for the future, too.

'Of course I have no way of knowing what Helen would have said about it all. Would she have agreed to a divorce? Who can say?'

'But she knew he had divorce in mind?'

'Oh, definitely. Though she never discussed it with me personally – we didn't have the opportunity. Besides, I hardly know her.'

'What seems rather curious to me,' said Hurst, scratching his back with his pencil, 'is the fact that Nigel Manson invited his mistress to spend a few days under the same roof as his wife.'

'Well, he was an artist, and all artists are eccentric. His recent success didn't help matters either – in fact, I'd say it made his behaviour all the more unusual. This house, for instance – neither Nathalie nor I had any idea the place existed until two days before our visit. He bought it and had it renovated in complete secrecy. A few weeks ago he invited us to spend the weekend with him, but wouldn't say where. He only let us know the address via telegram. What can you expect?' Holloway said with a rueful shrug. 'He had a childish side to him, and liked to spring surprises. Personally, I found it rather amusing. Nathalie, however, did not. You should have seen her! It took quite a bit of convincing to get her to come out here after that.'

'That's hardly surprising,' said Hurst with a sardonic smile. 'A few days under the same roof as your lover's wife doesn't sound particularly appealing.'

'I don't think that was it. She actually seemed to rather enjoy tormenting Helen with her butter-wouldn't-melt act. No, I rather think it was the fact that Nigel kept a secret from her that she found most bothersome. I'm quite sure she didn't come to the pub with us as a way of punishing him – usually, she can never say no to a captive audience. And of course, she's quite comfortable in the company of men.'

'She was angry at him?'

'Just a mild row, nothing more than that.'

'Did she have any other reason to be angry with him? Anything more serious?'

'Are you asking me whether she had a motive to murder him?' said Frank Holloway, clearly amused.

'If you like.'

'Not that I'm aware of. In fact, I'd say his death has cost her a great deal. She may not have been quite as infatuated with him as she was to begin with, but she was still dead set on marrying him. And apart from any sentimental or romantic considerations, I think she's going to lose out on a lot of money, too. Of course she'll still have a brilliant career ahead of her, but *The Invisible Man* was such a hit…'

'A hit,' said Hurst, 'which also made *you* a great deal of money.'

'Well, there's nothing unusual in that. As I told you, I took a lot of risks to get Nathalie where she is now.'

'So, Manson's death means that *you* will lose out on a lot of money, too?'

'I wouldn't go that far. For one thing, I'm not *his* manager. And we can always find another actor.'

'So, you don't have a motive either?'

'Not at all. In fact, I considered him a friend. And besides, I rather think I have a pretty solid alibi, don't you?'

'Well, the problem is that you *all* have solid alibis. So much so, in fact, that it makes the murder theory seem rather absurd. And that, Mr Holloway, brings us to the most extraordinary aspect of this entire story: everybody seems to be in agreement that Nigel Manson's death was caused by some kind of malevolent entity – a real-life invisible man!'

'And that's not all, Inspector,' said Holloway, toying with one of his signet rings. 'There's an old story about this place – about a woman who died after being pushed down the stairs by some kind of invisible creature…'

Archibald Hurst's rebellious forelock tumbled over his forehead once more as he exchanged a bewildered glance with Dr Twist.

13

The Magic Ring

'IT WAS A PAINFUL SITUATION. I COULDN'T bear it much longer. And yet… I still loved him.'

Helen Manson fell silent and dabbed at her eyes with a delicately-embroidered handkerchief. The day was beginning to wane behind the coloured panes of the large arched window, and shadows stretched across the landing. She turned away from them, sobbing quietly, and leaned against the balustrade. Her light sun-dress looked vaporous in the gloom.

The two detectives waited a moment, before Hurst cleared his throat and asked gently, 'So, would it be fair to say that you knew everything about your husband's relationship with Miss Marvel?'

'For a long time I told myself it was just gossip. But now I've had to face facts. I'd rather not talk about this any more.'

'I understand.' Hurst stepped forward and paused by Helen's side, peering down the staircase into the hall below. 'In that case, let's discuss the real reason we brought you here. Mr Holloway told us you might be able to shed some light on an old ghost story about this place.' Though his expression and tone were calm, the inspector was clearly eaten up by curiosity about this fresh and startling mystery.

'That's where the whole thing started,' said Helen Manson bitterly. 'Because it was that ghost story which gave Nigel the idea for the play. About a year ago, we were newlyweds and happened to drive past the house. Nigel stopped the car and a villager told us the story of a woman who was pushed down the stairs by an invisible man. That was the spur for Nigel – as soon as we got home, he started to write his play. But apart from the "invisible man" element, it has nothing in common with the story the old man told us.'

'One question, madam, if I may,' interrupted Dr Twist. 'You say that you happened to drive past this house. Were you on a sightseeing tour, or did you know the area?'

'I was born in Torquay, so I'd been to Dartmoor quite a bit. Not this area, though. And as for Nigel… Ah, it's coming back to me now. He told me he knew the area a little, since he'd travelled this way a few times. He wouldn't say any more, but the mysterious way he was acting makes me wonder if he had an old flame out here. In any case, he liked it here. Well, he must have done, since he bought this house – which, incidentally, he didn't tell me about until the beginning of last week.'

'From what I understand, he didn't tell anyone about it.'

Helen sniffed sadly. 'That's the way he was – a big kid who liked to spring surprises on people.'

'To your knowledge, did he have any enemies? Anybody who disliked him for whatever reason?'

'Nigel, enemies? Certainly not. Everybody loved him.'

'And yet…'

Helen shook her head desperately. 'This whole thing is horrible and incomprehensible. I still can't believe it. Sometimes I wonder if it's all just a nightmare.'

'I must ask you once again, madam, to please try to remember what exactly you saw. The key to the mystery may lie in your testimony. After all, you were closest to your husband when he fell…'

'But I've already told you a dozen times! I was about to head over and join Nigel at the window to try to catch a glimpse of this Professor Sitwell we were all waiting for. But then he started waving to Miss Marvel, which stopped me dead in my tracks.'

'Where exactly?'

'In front of the fireplace. And when he climbed out onto the window sill, I was rather embarrassed. After all, Dr Grant wasn't used to Nigel's eccentricities. I turned away, and then looked back towards Nigel. This was in the space of about five seconds. And then, all of a sudden, he was thrown forward…'

'Are you sure he didn't slip, or lose his balance?'

'I know that would explain everything, but it's not what happened. I'm quite sure of it. He didn't fall. He didn't topple. He didn't slip. He was *pushed*. It was awful. I tried to scream, but I couldn't make a sound. He was in the air for a split second, flailing with his arms to try to save himself… and then he was gone.'

'You also mentioned a draught, as though something moved past you. When did you notice that?'

'I think it was a little earlier, just after he called out to Miss Marvel. Colonel Weston questioned me about that at length. But you know how it is – when you start to think about something like that, you second-guess yourself, and wonder if it really happened at all.'

Hurst asked in a low voice, 'When you say "a draught," do you mean a gust of wind, or the feeling of someone moving past you?'

'I don't know. I can't remember. The more I think about it, the more doubts I have.'

'Well, I hope you appreciate the importance of whatever you have to say. But let's not dwell on it for the time being. So – you were looking directly at your husband when he fell, but not at Dr Grant.'

'Correct. I couldn't bring myself to look at him because of Nigel's acrobatics…'

'And Frank Holloway – did you hear him come in?'

'No.'

'No? When did you become aware that he was also present?'

'When he grabbed me by the shoulders and tried to calm me down. I was still screaming and shaking.'

'A few seconds after the tragedy, then?'

Her face betrayed a flicker of contempt. 'A few seconds, yes. I'd say about ten to be precise. I know you like accuracy, Inspector.'

'You ought to know, madam, it's that sort of accuracy that often leads to the truth,' Hurst stated in a firm and dignified manner. 'Which brings me to another question I doubt you will appreciate. All the same, I'm obliged to ask it. How much money does your husband leave you?'

'Money?' Helen repeated with a nervous laugh. 'Did you know he had to take out a loan to complete the renovations on this place? I doubt I'll get too much back from selling it. You'd better talk to my solicitor – he can give you a better idea.' She leaned against the balustrade again, her head in her hands to stifle the tears. 'The worst part of the whole thing,' she moaned, 'is that the very last image I have of him is the sight of him posing in the window, smiling down at that little hussy… And when he came home drunk the previous night, of course…'

Hurst cleared his throat. 'Very drunk, by all accounts.'

'What does it matter? And please don't tell me it's a question of accuracy.'

'Very well. By the way, what time was it?'

'About two in the morning. And he really was drunk – that much was obvious from what he said to me.'

'Oh? And what did he say?'

'Pure nonsense. Something about an "uncanny likeness," and "old friends"… and three dead girls. Completely incoherent.'

Dr Twist reflected for a few moments, then asked, 'Apart from that, was he in any particular frame of mind? Cheerful, sad, sullen?'

'Cheerful, naturally...' her brow suddenly furrowed. 'Now that you mention it, I remember he also looked rather puzzled, as though something was bothering him. But don't ask me what; I couldn't tell you. He reeked of alcohol, and he'd just woken me up. I wasn't in the mood to listen to any of his nonsense.'

'Very well,' said Hurst. 'And we still need to hear that famous story...'

Helen Manson's eyes gleamed strangely and her thin, pale lips curled in a smile. She stepped away from the railing and stood at the top of the stairs. 'Nearly fifty years ago, on a cold winter night,' she began solemnly, 'Madeleine Hall stood on the very spot where I am now... right before she met her fate.'

Hurst suppressed a shudder. There was something deeply sinister in the widow's voice. He had felt uncomfortable about following her into this wing of the house – even with Twist by his side. The last rays of daylight gave the gallery of ancestors along the walls an eerie, greenish tinge; their eyes seemed to glow and glare at him as he walked.

The longer the silence lingered, the more uncomfortable Hurst became. He jumped when Helen finally gave a sudden burst of laughter, full of despair and mockery. 'Oh God,' she said, 'I think I must be going mad. Forgive me. That's the way Nigel told the story on Saturday night, just before setting out for the pub with Frank Holloway. He wanted to frighten us – Miss Marvel and I – since we were going to be alone in the house. He was punishing us for refusing to join them. I already knew the story, of course, but it still gave me a chill when I heard it again. Well, here it is...

'Around fifty years ago, Sir Edward Hall – who owned this house – was a handsome fellow of about forty, suddenly widowed when his wife died in a riding accident. She'd given him two children – Celia, who was thirteen, and Arthur, who was two months old. After a decent interval, rumours began to circulate.

It was said that Sir Edward was planning to take a second wife, his housekeeper Agatha. She was a beautiful woman of about his own age, who cared for his house well and showed great affection for his children.

'But Sir Edward surprised everyone scarcely two months later by marrying a young woman from a nearby village. Her name was Madeleine. She was of good stock – or so it seemed – but there were still questions about her. Perhaps it was because of her remarkable beauty? Or the hasty marriage? "She's cast a spell on him," some people said. Or else, "She's only after his money." But one could hardly accuse her of neglecting her maternal duty. On the contrary, she adored the little baby, who was four months old by then. She doted on him. But all this devotion only attracted more gossip.

'The tragedy occurred one winter evening, a few days before Christmas. Madeleine was standing just where I am now, about to head down the stairs. But she paused for a moment to look at the snowflakes falling outside the window just there. At least, that's what the two witnesses said. Those witnesses were Agatha the housekeeper, who was about fifteen feet further along the corridor, and the chambermaid who was behind her. Suddenly, Madeleine's face froze in a mask of indescribable terror. And then she was hurled down the stairs, arms flailing, trying desperately to save herself.

'She fell all the way to the bottom, breaking her neck. Waiting for her downstairs were her husband and little Celia, who dropped her doll in fright. Sir Edward had just stepped in from the cold, and was still brushing the snowflakes from his clothes when he saw his new wife fall. But the little girl had watched her tumble all the way down from the upper landing. And while the house was dimly lit, she was certain there had not been anybody standing anywhere near to her young stepmother.

'This was confirmed by the housekeeper and chambermaid

upstairs. But they also swore their young mistress had not fallen by accident – that she was thrown, or pushed by a pair of invisible hands…'

There was a silence, and then it was Inspector Hurst who laughed. It was a forced laugh, with no hint of humour. 'Well, it seems as though all those witnesses jumped to their conclusions without any evidence.'

Helen gave him a veiled look. 'There was the ring. The ring they found on the landing.'

'A ring?' repeated Hurst, glancing helplessly at Dr Twist, who remained silent and thoughtful. 'What sort of ring?'

'An ordinary ring. Rather like a wedding ring. But you must understand this, Inspector: people in the village were convinced that Madeleine was a witch. And there's only one person powerful enough to rid the world of a witch. A person you can't see. A person who can make themselves as invisible as air simply by slipping a magic ring onto their finger…'

14

Vixina the Witch

That evening, Dr Twist and Inspector Hurst dined at the Red Lion. The inspector politely declined the landlord's offer of a private back room in which to enjoy their meal; they had not chosen the venue for its peace and quiet, but to study 'the lie of the land,' as Inspector Hurst put it. They were hoping to strike up a conversation with one or two regulars – specifically, Dr Thomas Grant, Professor Victor Sitwell, and Basil Hawkins. To that end, Twist and Hurst selected a vantage point in a corner at the far end of the bar.

The hum of general chatter grew quiet when they entered the room, and curious – even suspicious – glances were aimed in their direction. But as the regulars began to notice the amount of beer they quaffed, coupled with Dr Twist's voracious appetite, they realised that these were just two ordinary blokes after all. They were Londoners, but apart from that there was very little of interest about them.

'I don't like this one bit,' Hurst grumbled for the umpteenth time. 'I should have realised it was a trap! "You'll see, Archibald, the fresh Dartmoor air will work wonders for your sinuses!" That's the last thing the Superintendent said to me. I ought to have known straightaway – my health is the least of his concerns, except when he has an impossible mystery on his hands!'

Twist, who was gazing at a number of framed photographs

on the far wall, lit his pipe and replied, 'I'd say he knows a good detective when he sees one.'

'Please, for heaven's sake, no flattery!'

'You seem rather tense this evening, my friend.'

'Tense! Haven't I got good reason? We've already spoken to half the witnesses, and we haven't progressed an inch. In fact, the case is *more* complicated now; we have a new mystery on our hands which seems to rule out any hint of accidental death. I can see now why Colonel Weston was so hesitant to voice his opinion. No, I don't like this case at all, and something tells me there will be more surprises in store for us yet...'

'How strange,' said Dr Twist suddenly. He pointed to a vacant spot between the photographs. 'There appears to be one missing. See the faded patch?'

'You're right,' said a voice from close by. 'There was a picture there, until last Saturday.'

The two detectives turned to see the landlord, George Crawford. 'It was a picture that my wife and I happened to be very fond of. And I think I know who took it – it was somebody who came in with that actor, the one who died.'

'Is this the table they were sitting at?' asked Hurst.

'Yes, and getting absolutely plastered. I'd never seen Dr Thomas in that state before – I even had to help him get home. That's why I can't really bring myself to blame them too much. I reckon it was Victor Sitwell, because he told me early in the evening that the picture was really his. He was already a little tipsy, I think. I just pointed out that he was mistaken, but he kept on insisting. Finally I got him to admit that he might be mistaken, and that it was probably a duplicate of one he had at home. Anyway, I heard them talking about this photograph, and it must have been one of them who took it, because my wife noticed it was missing the following morning. Ah! Look, here come Professor Sitwell and Basil...'

Once the introductions were out of the way and the newcomers were seated at the table, the landlord returned to the subject of the photograph.

'George,' said Victor Sitwell, 'please stop pestering us about that! Basil, Thomas and I told you we didn't take it.'

'Then it was the actor or his friend…'

'I'd be very surprised. I remember that it was still on the wall when we got up to leave, and I don't really see…'

'Well, Alice and I were particularly keen on it because—'

'I'll give you mine, George. I promise it's exactly the same. Now, please, let's stop talking about it. Bring us a round of beer, would you?'

When the landlord returned with the drinks, the professor explained to the detectives that he, Basil and Dr Grant had first met Nigel Manson right here on the previous Friday. They became fast friends and arranged to meet the following evening to get to know one another better. Sitwell was about to recount the Saturday evening, but Hurst cut him short, explaining that his only concern was that they hadn't known each other before that Friday. Then he asked them both for their account of Manson's death.

Basil glanced at the professor, as though seeking permission, before launching into his story. It was of little use to the detectives, as he hadn't seen the victim before he hit the ground. He was around twenty yards away from the house when he heard the screams.

'So, Mr Manson invited you to visit along with the others?'

'He did,' said Basil, with a nod. 'Fortunately Professor Sitwell came to remind me on Sunday morning, otherwise I likely would have forgotten. He's so good to me. Honestly, without Professor Sitwell I don't know what I would do…'

'Please, Basil,' said the professor, 'just answer the inspector.'

'When you were walking out to the house,' continued Hurst, 'did you happen to meet anyone?'

'Well, I saw Professor Sitwell walking in front of me...'

'Anybody else?'

The question seemed to take Basil by surprise, and he hesitated for a second or two before turning to the professor.

'What's the matter, Basil?' asked the professor. 'Why don't you answer?'

'Well... Well, I saw David on the little path beside the road, near the manor...'

'David?' repeated Hurst. 'Who's he?'

'A shepherd,' Sitwell interjected. 'A young fellow – a bit of a wild one, as a matter of fact. David Lynder tends to go wherever he likes, whenever he likes. I wouldn't read too much into the fact that he was hanging around.'

'I wonder,' said Basil. 'I was watching him out of the corner of my eye on Saturday night. He was giving Mr Manson a very dirty look. Did you notice that, Professor?'

Sitwell cleared his throat uncomfortably. 'As a matter of fact... yes, I did notice. When he got up to leave, he looked in our direction, murmured something and then spat on the ground. Having said that, though, I wouldn't read too much into it, gentlemen. Lynder isn't much of a drinker, and it may simply be that he was a little inebriated, and so took a disliking to the first stranger he encountered...'

'Either way, we'll have a word with him when we get the chance,' said Hurst, making a note of it. 'All right, Professor Sitwell, your turn.'

Sitwell's account was meticulous and to the point – indeed Hurst considered it a masterpiece of the genre. 'It must have been just after three o'clock when I reached the gate at Trerice Manor. From there you can only see the roof clearly, but the rest of the house is occasionally visible between the trees. That's how I happened to see a figure sitting on the window sill. It's only sixty yards or so from the road to the house, and it was a clear and sunny day, so I could tell who it was without much difficulty. As I walked up the drive I wondered what he was up to, but when I started across the lawn I saw a young woman standing below the window. I didn't know who she was at the time, but the camera in her hand told me what Manson was up to. I was about thirty yards away when he fell. There are some large rhododendron bushes along the edge of the lawn which got in the way of the view, and besides, I didn't particularly focus on Manson because he didn't seem to have noticed me. Perfectly understandable, since he was looking down at the actress. That is, at the camera. And you could scarcely hear my footsteps.

'But I noticed immediately when he fell from the window. I had a perfect view, just above the rhododendrons. The brain tends to react in a split-second at times like that. For the briefest moment it looked as though he was suspended in mid-air, mouth gaping, eyes terrified, arms stretching out, desperately trying to save himself. While I didn't see the exact moment that he fell, it seems very unlikely to me that it happened by accident. He was obviously pushed, and I can swear that there was nobody behind him at the time – at least, no one who was visible in the window.

'It took me five or six seconds to run the rest of the way over to him. The girl was screaming beside the body. At her feet lay the camera she had just dropped – broken and ruined, just like its owner. And upstairs the other woman was screaming… there's not much else to say, is there?'

Hurst disagreed, before questioning the professor at length about the aftermath of the tragedy. But his information was of little use to the investigation. Therefore, Hurst guided the discussion towards the mysterious death of Madeleine Hall. 'We first heard of it only a couple of hours ago from Mrs Manson,' he explained.

'Everyone around here knows the story, Inspector. It's strange that nobody told you sooner,' Sitwell commented thoughtfully, chewing on an arm of his glasses.

'I agree.'

'Strange indeed. You were sent here to assist the local police, and yet they neglected to inform you of a mystery with obvious links to the present investigation.'

'We met Colonel Weston earlier this afternoon. Actually he *did* seem rather reserved – evasive, even. Anyway, I shall see him again tomorrow. In the meantime, can you tell us a bit more about it?'

Victor Sitwell took his time in lighting a cigar. 'The coroner's jury returned a verdict of accidental death, of course. That was no surprise. But I ought to point out that the ring which turned up on the landing actually belonged to Sir Edward, who had apparently lost it the previous day when he was taking it to be cleaned. At least, that's what he said. But one fact is certain – the ring did *not* make the wearer invisible. Several people experimented with it, to no avail.

'And Sir Edward never recovered from his misfortune. He became a hermit at the manor, and began losing his mind. But he lived long enough to hear of the death of his son Arthur in South Africa, following his sister Celia, who was apparently killed years before in a railway accident.'

Hurst nodded, then said, 'What I didn't quite understand was the story of the so-called magic ring and its connection to witchcraft. And besides, why did the villagers believe Madeleine Hall was a witch?'

'That I don't know. Perhaps it was just because it was considered indecent, and therefore suspicious, that she seduced a widower so soon after his wife's death? As for the ring, well...' Sitwell cracked a smile. 'You're obviously not from around here, otherwise you'd know the story of Vixina the Witch.'

Hurst frowned, but a glimmer of interest appeared in Dr Twist's eyes.

'Don't be afraid, it's only a legend,' said Victor Sitwell, before gesturing towards the bar. 'Same again, please, George. Now: Vixina the Witch was… Actually, Basil, you've been quiet for a little while, why don't *you* describe her for us?'

He complied with gusto, launching straight into the tale. 'She was the most hideous witch who ever walked on Dartmoor. Her face was wrinkled like a walnut, and covered with spots and warts, her hair was like straw, she had a long, hooked nose, her teeth were bright green and her breath was foul…'

'Excellent description, Basil!' Sitwell interrupted gleefully. 'And to make matters worse, her ugliness was surpassed only by her wickedness! She lived on one of the peaks near here – in fact, quite close to the Tavistock road – and near a marsh that would swallow anyone unfortunate enough to blunder into it. As soon as a passerby drew near to the spot, she would use her magic power to summon a thick fog. They would begin to get lost, and before long they would stray close to the marsh and she would simply push them into it.

'For many years, people travelling the area would fall victim to her diabolical trap, and the cursed place developed an evil reputation.

'That is, until one day, when a saviour arrived. He was a handsome young fellow who had done a good turn for some elves. In return, they had gifted him a magic ring that turned the wearer invisible. So, he was dispatched to rid the land of the dreaded witch.

'As soon as she saw him approaching, she enveloped him in a shroud of mist. However, slipping the magic ring onto his finger he managed to avoid the deadly quagmire and began to climb all the way to the rocky summit of the witch's lair.

'There he found the witch standing on the edge, peering down at the spot from which she had seen him disappear. All it took was a single push and she tumbled into the void so suddenly that she didn't have time to grab her broomstick. And she was dashed against the rocks below.'

'I see,' said Hurst with the delighted smile of a child who has just been told a thrilling bedtime story.

'England is full of myths and legends,' commented Dr Twist, 'but it seems to me that if one county were to be singled out for the top prize, it would be Devon. Because this *is* a legend, isn't it Professor Sitwell?'

'Of course it is. As I said, Vixina…'

'I'm not talking about Vixina. I'm talking about the invisible man who haunts Trerice Manor, and who murdered both Madeleine Hall and Nigel Manson.' Twist stared at the professor over the edge of his *pince-nez*. 'Surely you don't believe he *really* exists?'

At that moment the landlord returned, accompanied by Dr Thomas Grant, who greeted the detectives warmly. Sitwell pounced as soon as the doctor sat down, asking him to voice his own opinion in the matter of the invisible man.

Grant looked embarrassed, and gazed at his audience in perplexity. Then he said, in a rather feeble voice, 'Though I'm reluctant to admit it, it seems there can be little room for doubt. Sir Edward's wife at the end of the last century, then the three young women a few years ago, and now this young actor…'

'Three young women?' exclaimed Hurst, raising his voice so loud that the entire bar looked in his direction. 'Which young women?'

'Well, the ones who died…'

'Three young women died? How?' Hurst demanded, vainly tugging at his unruly forelock, trying to brush it back against his flushed forehead. 'And please, don't tell me they were pushed to their deaths by an invisible man.'

15

The First Lead

When Victor Sitwell finished recounting the tragic deaths of Eliza Gold, Constance Kent and Annie Crook, the other men at the table sat in silence. Dr Twist had remained expressionless throughout the story, leaning back in his chair with his arms folded, puffing on his pipe. Hurst, meanwhile, had grown paler and paler.

Stunned, he fixed his wild eyes on Sitwell and, after a few seconds, finally regained the power of speech. 'Three girls, murdered by an invisible man. Mysterious playing cards found at the scene of each crime. And a headless horseman who rides off into the night sky. What's next, Professor? The big bad wolf?'

'So,' observed Sitwell, 'I take it Colonel Weston hasn't mentioned any of this to you either?'

'No,' said the policeman curtly. 'He has not. But I have a feeling he'll be more talkative tomorrow. And he'll answer for his silence, you can bet on that. In the meantime...' he turned ferociously towards Basil and spoke in a menacing, slow voice, 'A headless horseman. Do you really expect me to believe that?'

'It's been nearly ten years now. And I'd been drinking a lot. But I swear to you, Inspector, that I saw a white horse gallop past me, with a rider on its back wearing a cloak, who had no head. And as it moved away, it flew higher and higher, till it eventually vanished into the sky.'

Hurst was on the verge of apoplexy. He closed his eyes, took a deep breath to calm himself, and managed to hold his tongue.

'Did this happen the night the first victim, Eliza Gold, disappeared?' asked Dr Twist calmly.

'Yes. And three days later she was found in the river.'

'And where exactly did you see this mysterious rider?'

'Well… I don't remember. I mean, I didn't know where I was at the time, either.'

Twist nodded thoughtfully, then looked at the professor. 'You've supplied the details, Professor Sitwell, but not your opinion.'

Victor Sitwell glanced at Basil Hawkins, then shrugged. 'I think you'd had too much to drink that night, Basil. The flying horse… seems a little much to me. I don't believe you're *lying*, Basil, I know you're an honest fellow. You probably *did* see a horse that night. But it must have been your mind that caused it to take flight…'

Hurst slammed the table with his fist. 'Damn it all to hell! Am I losing my mind? Or are we *all* losing our minds? At least the story of the invisible man had a kind of logic to it. But the playing cards, the headless horseman, the flying horse… none of it makes any sense!'

'That's where you're wrong, Inspector,' remarked Sitwell, contemplating his cigarette for a moment before lighting it. 'There's a direct correlation between the flying horse and the playing cards.'

Hurst was speechless, but Dr Twist observed mischievously, 'Would I be right in thinking there's another legend behind this?'

'Right you are. In fact, it's one of the best known tales in the region. The unfortunate hero is one Jan Reynolds, who sold his soul to the devil and found out the hard way that the prince of darkness does not take kindly to being tricked.

'It was an October evening – the twenty-first, to be precise

– in the year 1638. At St Pancras Church, in Widecombe-in-the-Moor, about twenty miles from here, the good reverend's sermon dragged on and on, while the unsuspecting Jan Reynolds sat among the congregation, dozing with a deck of playing cards in his hand.

'Suddenly, the church was shaken by a roaring thunderclap, and lit up by a bolt of lightning. Satan appeared, tethering his horse to the altar. Then he grabbed Jan Reynolds by the collar and hauled him away in a sulphurous cloud, vanishing as swiftly as he appeared.

'Not far from the local inn, four of Jan's cards fell to the ground and formed four patches of green known as "The Devil's Playing Cards" – each shaped like one of the four suits. And during the storm, the church was severely damaged, killing four people and seriously injuring many others. The details of this very real disaster are recorded on the wall of the church at Widecombe-in-the-Moor.

'And as for the headless horseman – they turn up everywhere in local legends. But I might add that very often the horse, too, has no head.'

'I think I shall lose *my* head if I hear any more of this,' grumbled Hurst. 'If I understand you correctly, Professor Sitwell, you are under the impression that three village girls sold their souls to the devil, only to displease Satan in some way, causing him to punish them by hurling them from a cliff and scattering a deck of playing cards in their wake as a warning to others?'

The professor shrugged. 'You said it made no sense. I was simply pointing out that it does, that's all.'

'Well, Professor,' said Dr Twist, 'surely you have your own opinion on the matter?'

Sitwell was silent for a moment before replying. 'After the third girl disappeared, my wife put forward a hypothesis which most of us – myself included – accepted as truth. While it doesn't explain everything, it seems fairly solid to me. And most of the facts support it.

'As I mentioned, shortly before each disappearance, the soon-to-be victim was full of cheer and *joie de vivre*. It was as if each of them was in love. And in all three cases, several witnesses indicate that they were – or seemed to be – accompanied by someone as they walked up to Wish Tor. Bearing in mind the time and place, we can assume it was the lover in question. Nothing unusual about that, of course. But the fact that in all three instances he not only failed to put in an appearance, but also to show the slightest concern about the missing girls, is quite bizarre. It makes one wonder if it was perhaps just one man – after all, the coincidence of three "fiancées" accidentally breaking their necks is so improbable that the likeliest explanation is a bizarre triple murder, carried out over three years. Three murders, coldly premeditated by a maniacal seducer – who likely came from one of the nearby villages.

'The problem is that nobody was ever able to determine who this diabolical Romeo was. Various conflicting testimonies arose. Rumours circulated. Most of the men in the village were under suspicion at one point or another – the young and the not-so-young. But the investigation was all the more difficult because it only focused on the third victim. You see, when Eliza Gold died it was believed to be an accident. The following year, when Constance Kent was found, people started to ask questions. But when Annie Crook disappeared, we couldn't help but notice how carefully this "suitor" of hers had concealed his identity.'

'Some suitor!' Dr Grant declared indignantly. 'Beast, more like. Servant of Satan!'

'Yes, servant of Satan…' Basil echoed with hatred in his eyes.

'Well, that seems logical enough to me,' said Hurst. 'But alas, it gets us no closer to solving the mystery. I immediately thought of a homicidal maniac while you were recounting the story, Professor. But it's the *invisibility* that I find bothersome! Because there can be no doubt about it – not after so many testimonies all saying the same thing. It was the second victim, wasn't it, who was seen standing alone by the cliff before she was pushed over the edge? And it wasn't just one witness but two, isn't that so? A pair of teenagers?'

'Indeed, two teenagers,' answered Sitwell. 'John and Betty – they are married now, with children.'

'And wasn't she also seen on her way up to the Tor, pausing by a tree to talk to someone, though no one was there? And as for the last one—' Hurst turned to Basil. 'You had a front row seat, isn't that right?'

Basil Hawkins nodded ruefully, then recounted as precisely as he could what he had witnessed that night. 'She was laughing and talking to someone, but she was walking up to Wish Tor all alone. When I realised she was in danger, I tried to call out to her, but I couldn't make a sound. I think it must have been the sheer panic, or else I'd just drunk too much... maybe both. In any case, I'll never forget the sight of that poor girl walking cheerfully off into the night, never suspecting for a moment that she was going to her death. And there was nothing I could do about it...' he added, wringing his hands.

Disheartened, Hurst scratched his head. 'All this is beyond me. What's the connection between the deaths of these three young women, the death of Madeleine Hall fifty years earlier *and* the death of Nigel Manson? For God's sake, what sort of creature are we dealing with here?'

'A diabolical one,' murmured Victor Sitwell. 'There can be no doubt about it.'

Dr Grant and Basil nodded gravely.

'Professor Sitwell,' Dr Twist asked suddenly, 'would you mind writing down the story you have just told us? And perhaps include any events which occurred in the village that strike you as important or out of the ordinary?'

'Certainly. It's quite easily done – I made extensive notes at the time. Feel free to stop by my house and pick them up whenever you like. Tomorrow, perhaps, at teatime?'

Dr Twist accepted the invitation gratefully.

After that, Inspector Hurst questioned Dr Grant about the defenestration of Nigel Manson.

'No, I didn't feel a draught. Not that I can recall, anyway. He wasn't in the centre of my vision because of the angle of the chair, but I could see his silhouette. Anyway, I'm quite certain there was nobody anywhere near him when he fell.'

'What was Mrs Manson doing at that moment?' Hurst asked, notebook and pencil in hand.

'She was in front of the fireplace.'

'And what was she doing?'

'She had a statuette in her hands. And I think she was looking at her husband.'

'You think so?'

'She appeared to be facing that way. But as I said, I wasn't looking precisely in that direction.'

'Did you see Mr Holloway open the door?'

'Um… no.'

'You mean to say that when Nigel Manson fell, there wasn't anybody coming through the doorway?'

'No, all I'm saying is that I wasn't looking that way either. My eyes were fixed on the bottles of liqueur on the table in front of me.'

'Did you hear the door opening?'

'No, not that I can recall. But my hearing isn't what it used to be.'

'At what point, then, did you become aware of Mr Holloway's presence in the room?'

'Let me see… Mrs Manson froze for a very brief moment, then she screamed and dashed over to the window. I got up from my seat, and that's when I saw Mr Holloway come scurrying past me to join Mrs Manson.'

The inspector did not pursue this line of questioning further, and concluded the interview there. He and Dr Twist said their goodnights shortly after that; they did not linger on the landing, and the look that passed between them before they parted ways was decidedly unoptimistic.

Once Alan Twist was secluded in his room, he decided to sit up for one last pipe of a very long, tiring day. He opened the window and leaned out as he smoked. Below him, the downstairs bay windows cast long pools of light towards the surrounding trees. The wild expanse of Dartmoor was swallowed by the darkness, its silence only broken by the ripple of a nearby stream. The rising wind carried a distant lamb's bleat.

Dr Twist was suddenly seized by a deep melancholy. He wasn't sure whether it was caused by his surroundings, or by the insoluble nature of the case. He and Hurst had worked together on many bizarre and seemingly impossible mysteries in their time, but this particular investigation felt more like a fairy tale than a murder inquiry. He had been quietly confident when he first arrived at Trerice Manor, albeit rather troubled by the initial eyewitness testimonies, and then surprised to learn about the strange death of Madeleine Hall and its bizarre similarity to the fate of Nigel Manson. But the circumstances had continued to grow stranger and stranger. He was quite literally baffled. It seemed impossible for all those eyewitnesses to be mistaken, no matter how incredible the facts might seem. Naturally he had spotted several clues – including one particularly blatant lie in one of the accounts which might prove significant – and yet the whole case felt too amorphous and vague, a dark mishmash of folklore, and for the first time in his career he feared his deductive powers were letting him down.

He was deep in thought when there came a knock at the door.

'Come in,' he called, and, without so much as turning round, said to his visitor, 'I gather you are having trouble sleeping as well, Archibald?'

The stout figure that had entered the room closed the door gently before replying. 'Indeed, but I think it might prove to be a blessing. You see, I was just running through everything we heard today in my head, and I remembered something Mrs Manson told us which I think might be important. You remember her husband's "incoherent rambling" when he came back from the inn on Sunday night?'

'Naturally. He mentioned "three dead girls" – that's what you're referring to, isn't it? And what do you make of it, Archibald?'

'This: Nigel Manson was murdered because he found out who killed those three girls.'

16

A Walk on Wish Tor

THE FOLLOWING MORNING THE SKY WAS GREY, but a sweeping wind promised brighter spells to come. It was eleven o'clock when the first ray of sunlight found its way into the drawing room of Trerice Manor, bringing with it Colonel Weston. After greeting the two detectives who waited for him, he produced from his wallet a photograph which was unmistakably the last image of Nigel Manson.

The open window took up roughly half of the photograph, giving Twist and Hurst a clear and focused shot of Manson himself. His position on the window sill was exactly as described by the eyewitnesses. He looked relaxed and secure where he sat – the idea of him slipping or falling accidentally seemed even less likely. The grin on his face refuted the suicide theory. Apart from that, the picture had very little to tell them.

'It's a shame it isn't a wider shot,' commented Twist. 'It might tell us a bit more. And it's even more of a shame it wasn't taken a second or two later. But you're right, Colonel, it's not much use to us. Not that I expected much – it would have been too good to be true.'

Hurst looked from the photograph to Colonel Weston. 'By the way, we learned quite a bit more yesterday, after you left…' Then he treated the colonel to a brief, reproachful summary of the facts.

When he was finished, Weston nodded vaguely. 'So, now you

see the full magnitude of the problem. The only reason I didn't tell you the whole story yesterday was to avoid influencing your judgement. Now you have the full context for the mystery. The inquest has been postponed for a few days; it's now going to take place next week. And, like the deaths of those three girls, not to mention the death of Madeleine Hall, it's very likely the jury will return a verdict of accidental death. Unless…' He fixed his eyes on Hurst. 'Unless you manage to clear up the matter beforehand. You ought to know that your superintendent is a friend of mine, Inspector. He speaks very highly of you. He says you can explain miracles…'

'Well, let's not exaggerate…' said Hurst, flushing with pride.

'I'm not exaggerating. He assured me over the telephone that he had a man who could "explain miracles". Those were his exact words.'

'"Miracle" is an apt description, anyway,' Hurst remarked. 'How else to describe a flying horse and an invisible killer?' Frowning, he paced up and down in front of the fireplace, before returning to face Weston. 'Anyway, we must tackle the problem head-on. Methodically, of course. That's what my associate and I did this morning, before you arrived – we focused solely on the death of Nigel Manson, and nothing else for the moment. Twist, I'll let you run through the conclusions we've reached so far.'

'In addressing the mystery,' Twist began, 'we eschewed every preconception except for the murder hypothesis. That is to say, this was a murder committed by a flesh-and-blood human, using some sort of diabolical method to achieve their ends. And we focused particularly on the material aspects of the crime. By which I mean, we did not examine psychological or emotional considerations for the time being.

'We soon concluded that the crime could only have been committed from one of two very specific locations: either this very room, or somewhere outside the window. We started with this room. There were two people in here when Manson fell, plus a third – Mr Holloway – who claims to have been on his way through the doorway at the crucial moment. I say "claims" because we only have his word for it – the other two witnesses are completely positive that he was not in the room *before* the fall. We have therefore provisionally ruled out Mr Holloway, because in order to commit the murder he would have needed to do so from somewhere outside of here. That would have left him only ten seconds or so – at the absolute maximum – between the fall and his approach to comfort Mrs Manson by the window.

'Dr Grant and Helen Manson were sitting in an armchair in the centre of the room and standing by the fireplace, respectively. This is confirmed by their own testimonies, and by that of Mr Holloway – which is important, because without it we would be forced to conclude that one of them was responsible for the murder. At the fatal moment neither person was paying much attention to the other, and it may have been a single, apparently innocuous gesture that caused the fall. This leaves us with the following question: *how* might Dr Grant or Helen Manson have successfully pushed Nigel Manson out of the window with a single, barely noticeable movement? The only idea that springs to mind is the use of a pole, or a long stick, to somehow tip him over into the void. But this doesn't hold up, of course. Even assuming such an object exists, how did the killer come by it? And how did they conceal it afterwards? And, most damning of all, how did they ensure nobody was watching them at the crucial moment?'

There followed a long silence, after which Weston declared that it seemed absolutely impossible, just like every other proposed solution.

So, the trio descended the stairs and ventured outside, positioning themselves in a spot directly below the window. Once again, it was Twist who spoke. 'And if we assume that the crime was committed from outside, then it would seem that the victim should have been "pulled" rather than pushed. But how? Bearing in mind all the other established conditions, the only possibility I can propose is that of a thin, very strong and inconspicuous thread, like a fishing line. But then, it would have to be thrown manually! Any other weapon, like a harpoon or a lasso, would have been much too obvious.'

Twist looked around the garden. 'But then,' he continued, 'another problem presents itself. There is nothing – not even a tree – directly in front of the window. But the operation would need to have been perpetrated at tree-height, since all the witnesses describe Manson falling "forward." The closest locations are the two windows perpendicular to those of the drawing room. Specifically, the window in Frank Holloway's room, or the one in the upstairs passageway. But in either case, surely the victim would have been seen to topple sideways, rather than forward? And surely he would have just fallen vertically, rather than lurching forwards, if the assailant was down here...'

'Miss Marvel, you mean?' put in Weston. 'The trouble is, Victor Sitwell wasn't far away, and saw her snapping the photograph of her lover. And even if she *had* managed to launch an invisible thread in a moment or two when the professor's view was obscured, how could she have detached and hidden it before he came running over?

'It couldn't have been a rigged camera, either. Although it was smashed to bits, we were able to examine it thoroughly and found that it was just an ordinary camera, with no added gimmicks or devices. Nothing suspicious about it whatsoever, in fact.'

'Besides,' put in Hurst, 'how could one end of the wire have been attached to the victim? By a noose hanging from the window sill? Or by a hook attached to his clothes?'

Weston shook his head. 'Impossible. We checked the dead man's clothes inch by inch, not to mention his entire body, and there were no suspicious marks or tears. The idea did cross my mind too, you know. We also thought of a loose brick in the window sill which might have been pulled violently, causing it to dislodge and Manson to lose his balance. But then again,' he added irritably, 'it's the *way* he fell which is causing us so many problems.'

Twist was similarly annoyed. His lips tightened before he spoke. 'You're quite right, Colonel. None of this adds up. It *did* occur to me that the culprit might have been operating from one of the upstairs windows I previously mentioned. After all, Miss Marvel had a clear view of what was going on, but she was only looking through the camera's viewfinder. In other words, her field of vision was greatly restricted. And even the slightest speck of dust on the lens might have obscured a thin length of fishing wire. That is, until she lowered the camera, at which point she would have seen everything. And so would Professor Sitwell. No, I'm afraid we are on the wrong track. Perhaps we ought to have lunch, to replenish our little grey cells?'

They ate at the inn in Stapleford, all the while talking of the 'invisible man'. Although truthfully Dr Twist merely listened – he was determined to do justice to George Crawford's cooking, which he positively devoured, much to the landlord's delight. The other two investigators posited just about every conceivable hypothesis. These were as plentiful as they were unconvincing.

Disappointed, Hurst stubbed out his cigar in his mashed potato. 'No man has ever managed to turn himself invisible. It's impossible, and always will be. There *must* be another explanation.'

Twist gazed forlornly at the mashed potato with its protruding cigar stub.

'Another explanation, yes. But what *manner* of explanation?' said Weston with a sigh.

'Just what do you mean by that?' asked Twist.

'You gentlemen aren't from around here, so you can't be expected to know everything about the place. But Dartmoor is not London,' Weston added sententiously. 'I'm a local boy, so I know the history of the area quite well. Not as well as Professor Sitwell, of course…'

'How curious,' Twist observed. 'Now that you make the comparison, I notice something else you have in common with Professor Sitwell and his friends. Not *defeatism* exactly, but shall we perhaps call it… a dearth of optimism about the outcome of our investigation?'

'My point exactly,' sighed Weston. 'You're not from around here. Otherwise you'd know already that some phenomena simply can't be explained. Do you really think all our local legends are entirely baseless? There's a kernel of truth in every story, believe me. And besides, Dartmoor is unlike anywhere else on earth. The various tragedies of Stapleford attest to that. There's an explanation for everything, Inspector, but perhaps not the type of explanation you are accustomed to dealing with. I'm sure this will be uncomfortable listening for two Londoners, but let me remind you gentlemen – things are very different here.'

There was an uncomfortable silence. 'Our ignorance of certain supernatural phenomena might seem to support your explanation, Colonel,' said Dr Twist. 'But I'm quite certain the "demon" who pushed Nigel Manson from that window is as human as you or I, and also happens to be responsible for the fate of those three unfortunate young women. All right, let's set aside Nigel Manson's death for a moment and return to what happened here ten years ago…'

It was two o'clock in the afternoon when the three men left the inn. The sun was high in the sky, the air was warm, the surrounding fields were green and peaceful. They walked past whitewashed cottages dotted along the lanes, all within the benevolent gaze of the church steeple…

'Come on, Twist,' said Hurst. 'We're not here to daydream.'

Twist, who had lingered a moment to appreciate the landscape, nodded and went with them.

'I'll take you up to Wish Tor,' declared Weston, 'but then I'm afraid I shall have to leave you. Now, getting back to the topic at hand – I was well aware of the rumours Sitwell told you about. We conducted our own discreet investigations into the matter. I say "discreet" because you must understand that the slightest hint of suspicion directed towards one of the local lads and the other villagers would have closed ranks. Anyway, we were never able to identify this mysterious "seducer". We collected several statements indicating that Annie Crook seemed to have developed a crush on somebody before her death, but no one could tell us who the object of her affections might be, or even provide the vaguest description. As for the other two dead girls, obviously there was nothing doing there either. Having said that, I'm inclined to believe we were on the right track. Whoever this mysterious Romeo was, I reckon he murdered those three girls. But as for your theory that Nigel Manson was killed because he found out the fellow's identity… I'm not so sure. Where did that idea come from?'

'Nowhere specific,' Hurst answered, with a little cough. 'It's… an idea, as you say. Perhaps tomorrow we shall have a better one.'

Within five minutes, Weston took his leave of the pair, directing Twist and Hurst along the path towards the summit of Wish Tor. The incline was rather gentle for the first thirty yards or so, but it grew considerably steeper as they progressed. Hurst was soon panting and sweating profusely, all the while cursing Twist, who strode ahead briskly, in spite of the three hefty portions he had consumed at lunch. When they reached the summit, Hurst sat down on a large rock while Twist examined the surrounding area.

'A remarkable place,' Twist commented as he continued his

investigation. 'The path is uneven and scattered with boulders, but up here is a smooth plateau – quite a rarity on granite formations like this! Take a look around, Archibald. The view is splendid! Enjoy it, my friend. You'll find nothing like this in London. The air is incomparable, and the peace and quiet is wonderful. Even, dare I say it, inspirational.'

'Don't forget the babbling brook…' said the inspector sardonically.

'You mean that crystalline murmur, like something from Vivaldi's "Four Seasons"? Ah! *This* must be where John and Betty were when they saw Constance Kent! I wouldn't call it a "cave" exactly, it's only a few feet deep. Come and have a look, my friend.'

'In a minute. Let me catch my breath.'

'Take your time. Let's pretend it's dark, and picture the scene as the professor described it. So, the two youngsters are over there, and here comes Miss Kent along the same path we took. She looks perfectly cheerful. She's humming to herself and calls out several times, "Hello? Where are you?" Then she stops here.'

Twist emerged from the little cave and zigzagged between rocks to the very edge of the cliff. He stopped dead, tilting his head very slightly to get a look below.

With difficulty, Hurst got up and joined him. He was startled by the sheer drop of about a hundred feet onto a bed of sharp rocks, over which the waters of the stream tumbled en route to the village.

'She was here,' Twist continued. 'Right on this spot, looking down at this same view. Quite a height, isn't it? Do you think we'd have the slightest chance of survival if we fell from here? It would be a miracle, wouldn't it? No, I'd say a fall from this height would mean certain death. Can you imagine her terror when she felt those two invisible hands on her back, pushing her over into the void?'

17

The Vanishing Photograph

Hurst turned sharply, scanning his surroundings for some invisible enemy.

'Better safe than sorry,' he said with a scowl.

'For a chap who claims not to believe in the supernatural, I must say your behaviour is rather odd.'

'Then don't bother spouting these tired old ghost stories. Because that's exactly what you were doing, and clearly loving every minute of it. Now: why don't we head back down?'

They retraced their steps to the village, then crossed the stone bridge over the stream and followed its meandering path to the foot of Wish Tor. Dr Twist gazed dreamily at his surroundings, lost in idle contemplation of the water tumbling from stone to stone, foaming and sparkling like a cascade of sunlight.

'It hasn't rained much lately,' he commented, 'and you'll notice the water level is rather low. But don't be fooled – all it takes are a few rainstorms to transform this babbling brook into a raging torrent.'

'I never said otherwise,' the inspector grumbled.

Twist leaned back to study the ominous silhouette of the Tor against the azure sky.

'Of course. I'm simply pointing out the likelihood that the three young women were swept a great distance from here by the current. That's what I was attempting to verify. It has now been verified.'

Archibald Hurst produced a handkerchief from his pocket and dabbed his sweat-streaked forehead. Then he consulted his watch. 'It's getting hot, and we're not seeing Sitwell until teatime. What shall we do until then?'

'We should rest for a couple of hours, Archibald. Two whole hours of strolling around, admiring the scenery, breathing the fresh air… we'll be utterly refreshed, you'll see!'

At a quarter to five, the two detectives approached the hedge-lined property belonging to Victor Sitwell. Hurst, his wild forelock still very much in evidence, bustled impatiently beside Twist, who whistled cheerily as he pushed open the garden gate.

About halfway along the path, beside one of the flowerbeds, they spotted Basil Hawkins. He wore an apron and straw hat, and was clearing away his gardening tools. He seemed delighted to see the two visitors, and began to explain his duties here at the professor's house, emphasising Sitwell's kindness towards himself and so many other villagers. While Dr Twist studied the gardener discreetly from behind his *pince-nez*, Hurst gazed admiringly around the property, his eyes finally settling on the rosebushes.

'You've certainly done the professor proud,' he commented. 'Those rosebushes alone are proof of that.'

'Well… as a matter of fact, the rosebushes are the only thing I *don't* touch. The professor takes care of them himself. He has a passion for roses and…' Spotting Twist's thoughtful expression, he said, 'Is something wrong, sir?'

'No, it's nothing. You just reminded me of someone, that's all. By the way, you're not from around here, are you?'

A shadow crossed Basil's features and he murmured, 'No, I'm not.'

There was a strange silence, finally broken by Hurst impatiently declaring, 'By the way, there's something we need to ask you about Saturday night. Think carefully before you answer, because this is very important. Was there any point during the evening when Nigel Manson mentioned the three dead girls?'

Basil considered this for a moment, rubbing his chin, then said, 'Now that you mention it, yes he did...'

Before he could say any more, Mrs Sitwell appeared at the front door to invite the detectives inside.

The clock struck five as their benevolent hostess served tea and sandwiches in the sitting room. 'My husband should be here any moment,' she said with a smile. 'In the meantime, here's something to keep your strength up.'

Hurst politely informed her that they were in no hurry, and that their time was considerably less valuable than the professor's – especially considering all his good deeds around the village.

Blushing, Mrs Sitwell tried to downplay the gardener's lavish praise of her husband. Dr Twist made short work of the sandwiches while Hurst looked on in amusement. Eventually, their conversation turned to the circumstances in which Mrs Sitwell had first met her husband-to-be.

'I'll never forget it,' she said. 'He was twenty-five at the time, and living in a cottage in Bodmin. I was there on holiday with my aunt. We happened to bump into one another on the first day of the tin miners' strike...'

The conversation was interrupted by the arrival of the gentleman in question, and talk soon turned to other matters. Within half an hour, Florence Sitwell left them and Hurst returned to the question he had asked Basil Hawkins in the garden. Sitwell had just fetched a file containing his notes on the three young victims. Like Basil, he froze for a moment in thought. Then he snapped his fingers. 'Yes, of course! We *did* talk about it. It was because of the photograph... Did you happen to see the noticeboard in the pub? The one with all the photographs pinned to it: football teams, wedding parties, cricket matches and the like. Ah, of course, you heard George accuse me of nabbing one of them… Well, at some point during Saturday evening, I happened to remark that the photograph was mine. It did *look* like one of mine and, in fact, I do have the same one here at home. But I'm afraid I was starting to feel the effect of the beer.

'Anyway, George came over and told me I was mistaken, and we argued back and forth for a few minutes before I eventually gave in. And he's right; it *was* his. He was especially attached to it because it was the only one he had which showed his adopted daughter, Annie Crook.

'It was taken at the village fete and – as luck would have it – shows all three of the victims in the foreground: Annie Crook, Eliza Gold and Constance Kent. That was a few months before Eliza Gold was found in the stream.

'I had the picture in my hand as I discussed it with George, and happened to mention the three girls. Nigel Manson and his friend pricked up their ears, as most people do when they hear the story for the first time. I would say Manson was more curious about it than Holloway, but I can't be sure. Anyway, we started chatting about the case. But that reminds me… at one point, Manson picked up the photograph and examined it for quite a while. He seemed confused and rather quiet. He looked at it two or three more times during the evening. But I don't think there's any more I can tell you, I'm afraid.'

Hurst and Dr Twist exchanged a thoughtful look, and then Hurst advanced his theory about the motive for Nigel Manson's murder. 'And what you've just told us,' he concluded, 'seems to confirm our hypothesis. Something – or rather, someone – in the picture caught his eye. According to his wife, in spite of his drunkenness, he was clearly disturbed about something when he got back to the manor on Saturday night. It's a safe bet, Professor Sitwell, that the killer of those three young women is somewhere in that photograph. Can you remember who else is in it?'

Victor Sitwell removed his spectacles and sighed. 'Almost half the village… Well, a good part of it, anyway. Who exactly was in the picture? I couldn't say for sure. The easiest thing to do would be to look at it for yourselves, since I also have a copy.'

Sitwell excused himself and left the room. After five minutes, he returned looking irritated. 'Whenever you're desperate to lay your hands on something, you can bet it will disappear. I'm afraid I can't find the photograph. Florence thinks it must be in the attic, which means it will take a little while to ferret out. But I shall get to it as soon as possible, gentlemen, since I know how important it is. I have some time tomorrow afternoon, so I'll go through the attic with a fine-tooth comb. As soon as I have the picture, I shall bring it over to you.'

'That would be most appreciated, Mr Sitwell,' said Hurst with ill-concealed frustration. 'Like you say, it's very important.'

'The missing photograph *is* rather curious,' murmured Dr Twist, lost in thought. 'The one from the inn, I mean.'

'Well, either way, none of us took it,' Sitwell asserted. 'I promise you that, since I put it back on the board myself after we were finished with it.'

'But the next morning,' Twist said dreamily, 'it was gone. Curious indeed.'

18

The Young Shepherd

ON LEAVING THE HOUSE, HURST AND DR TWIST caught up with Basil, who was just on his way out through the garden gate. Unfortunately, he was unable to supply further detail, but he did confirm the professor's account almost to the letter.

Within half an hour, the two detectives were back in the drawing room of Trerice Manor. Hurst stood before the fireplace, pontificating about this latest development with sweeping gestures and verbal flourishes, keeping Helen Manson, Nathalie Marvel and Frank Holloway rapt with suspense.

'But,' he concluded, 'what exactly did he see in that photograph? Alas, I don't know. But it was a very specific detail. Most likely the face of the murderer, though we cannot say for sure. It could have been some other form of clue. Regardless, it must have been Professor Sitwell's description of the case coupled with that mysterious "something" in the photograph which caused a click of recognition in his mind. What do you think, Mr Holloway? Were you with him at the time?'

'I was, and yes, everything Professor Sitwell has told you is accurate. Personally, I wasn't paying too much attention to the story of these three girls, or to Nigel for that matter. But he certainly seemed captivated by the story. And then he picked up the photograph again to examine it…' The impresario fell silent, an index finger raised thoughtfully to his lips. His signet rings glittered in the light of the low-hanging chandelier overhead.

'You were saying?' prompted Hurst.

'According to your theory, Inspector, Nigel Manson was targeted by the murderer because he realised that Nigel could identify him. Which means he must have been watching Nigel at the moment inspiration struck. In other words, the murderer was at the inn that evening.'

'You're beginning to catch on,' said Hurst. 'You see now that it wasn't mere chance that the murderer happened to spot Nigel looking at the photograph. In fact, his ears must have pricked up as soon as the conversation turned to the three murdered girls. Then, he likely started to eavesdrop on your little party. With that in mind, please do your very best to remember, sir. Try to remember exactly what Mr Manson said on that subject the next day. Even the smallest reference or vague allusion could be vital. We can't afford to miss a single detail.'

'The next day?' repeated Frank Holloway doubtfully. 'Personally, I'm not aware of anything.'

Helen Manson and Nathalie Marvel concurred.

'When I say "the next day,"' Hurst explained, 'I really mean any point following his return to the house. When you got back from the inn, for instance.'

Holloway gave a nervous laugh. 'I was in quite a state, as you know. All I really remember is him walking up to the wrong room… when he…' Glancing at the young actress, he cleared his throat, apparently both self-conscious and rather amused by the memory.

The blood drained from Nathalie Marvel's face and she chewed her lip before interrupting. 'When he came into my room, yes. He was completely drunk, and…' Her voice pitched up slightly. 'Do you really want to know what he had to say to me?'

She glared defiantly at the inspector for a moment before turning to Helen Manson, who looked so frail in her armchair, and said weakly, 'That won't be necessary.'

'He was very drunk,' the actress continued, 'and what he said to me has nothing whatsoever to do with this case.'

'Very well,' said Hurst, eager to avoid any emotional conflict that might derail his inquiry. 'But what about you, Mrs Manson? Bearing in mind what we now know, surely you can provide further detail? Among his drunken ramblings that night didn't he say anything else about the "curious resemblance" and the "three dead girls"?'

'I really don't remember, I'm afraid. But I shall give it some thought, and perhaps something else will come to me…'

Hurst's patience was reaching its ebb. A vein in his temple had begun to throb dangerously. 'This is getting us nowhere,' he muttered. 'At least we'll have Sitwell's copy of the photograph soon – the day after tomorrow at the latest.'

Frank Holloway smiled innocently. 'By the way, Inspector, how is the rest of the investigation going? I mean, the murder itself? Have you got anywhere with the problem of the invisible assassin?'

Hurst glared. 'No.'

'How curious. Because it seems you are now pursuing more rational explanations.'

'Does that surprise you? You believe in ghosts, Mr Holloway? Mind you, it seems that everyone in this place believes in demons, devils, witches, goblins, headless horsemen and the like. And not just the drunkard Basil or George the innkeeper, but the professor, the doctor, even the chief constable! They don't admit it outright, of course, but they insist that one must be "careful with such things."'

There was a silence, finally broken by Dr Twist. 'We've made no progress in this matter. Not even the beginnings of a rational explanation.'

'And Inspector,' said Frank Holloway, 'when are you planning to let us go home?'

'You're not prisoners,' Hurst snapped. 'All I ask is that you stay for another day or two if you are able.'

Helen Manson didn't comment, but stared blankly out of the window – the same window from which her husband had fallen four days earlier. Holloway, meanwhile, glanced questioningly at Nathalie, who declared that she would remain until the investigation was complete.

Twist suddenly exclaimed, 'Good heavens, half-past six already! We'd better leave now, Hurst, or we'll be late for dinner. Whatever would George think of us?'

That evening, Hurst and his companion dined in a private room. Now that they had some time to take stock of their findings, discretion was vital.

'We've only been here two days,' said Twist, discreetly eyeing the inspector's uneaten fruit salad, 'but it feels like weeks. Things looked very different when we were in London, wouldn't you say, Archibald?'

'I'm afraid so. I was certain that Manson had simply slipped and fallen by accident, and that all the uncertainty surrounding the incident was just because of conflicting testimonies and the apparent similarities to his play *The Invisible Man*. When I began to consider the possibility of murder, I told myself that the culprit had to be one of the three people in his immediate social circle; namely his wife, his mistress and her manager. And that the killer must have used some sort of theatrical gimmick to pull off the murder in broad daylight. Of course, that didn't last long.'

'We had no idea what other surprises lay in store for us. But have faith, Archibald. Soon we will find the thread that ties it all together. I skimmed through the notes Sitwell provided; they are a marvel of precision. I shall read them in full tonight. I'll be damned if the answer isn't in there somewhere. In the meantime, if you don't mind, I'd like to review the case in chronological order, so we can piece together all these disparate mysteries in the light of our most recent discoveries.

'So: roughly twenty years prior to the turn of the century, a young woman fell to her death from the staircase in the east wing of Trerice Manor. Three independent witnesses — not including her husband — confirm this was no accident, but that she was pushed by "invisible hands". Rumours abound that the dead woman was a witch, and there is also a local legend of a witch-hunter with a magic ring that turns the wearer invisible.

'Fifty years later, a young woman disappears from the village and turns up drowned several days later. A deck of playing cards is found on her body. This incident is deemed to be an accident — save for the curious detail of a headless horseman, which was seen taking flight at the time of the disappearance.

'The following year, a second young woman is found dead in the same body of water, at the same time of year. Cards are found scattered over the surrounding fields. However, this time there are two witnesses who claim to have seen the victim pushed — I repeat, *pushed* — from the edge of a rocky outcrop when she was clearly alone. And some time before that, a different witness spotted her walking up to the Tor while chatting to someone who wasn't there; an invisible companion.

'Another year later, a third young woman goes missing. She is also seen walking up to that accursed tor, talking and laughing with an invisible man. A deck of playing cards will subsequently be found in a field close to the stone bridge over the stream. These playing cards suggest another local legend, which happens to involve the devil himself.

'A few more years pass. One day, a man is travelling through the area and learns the tragic tale of Madeleine Hall. This inspires him to write a stage comedy, which becomes a huge hit. He buys the manor house that made him famous, and moves in… only to be hurled from an upstairs window by an invisible man, just like the creature in his play.'

Hurst pushed away the fruit salad and said, 'That's quite a tale. Would you like my dessert, Twist? I haven't touched it – this business has ruined my appetite.'

'Your what? Oh, of course! We wouldn't want to offend George, would we?'

Within moments, the salad bowl was empty and the two detectives decided to return to the main bar for coffee.

As he served them, George discreetly indicated a young man of impressive physical build, who was dressed rather shabbily. 'That's the shepherd, David Lynder. You were wanting to speak to him, weren't you?'

Hurst thanked the landlord and eyed the sturdy, dark-haired fellow for a moment. Then he looked slyly at Twist. 'I'd almost forgotten him. He's the chap who was staring so venomously at Nigel Manson, remember? And Basil saw him prowling near Trerice Manor not long before the murder. He's handsome, too; I can imagine the girls swooning over him. This could be our man, Twist. Now, go and find us a table; I'll be with you shortly. I'm going to invite him to join us.'

Within a couple of minutes David Lynder was sitting with them, looking wary as he clutched a foamy half-pint of beer. His eyes moved constantly between Dr Twist and Inspector Hurst, and seemed aglow with hatred as soon as the name 'Nigel Manson' cropped up. Hurst had expected this reaction – in fact he had been hoping for it – but even he was surprised at the young man's vehemence.

'The devil has reclaimed one of his own,' Lynder commented darkly.

'I beg your pardon?' said Hurst, his eyes wide. 'I'm not sure what you mean…'

'I mean exactly what I said. That fellow was a demon with the ladies – I knew it as soon as I saw him. Not that I saw much of him, mind you, but I'll never forget his face. It was a long time ago, but I remember it like it was yesterday. I was in love with Eliza back then, and he stole her from under my nose, right here in this room. He'd never even been in here before, not even once. And then a year later he did the same thing with Constance, the bastard!'

'Eliza? Constance?' Hurst echoed. 'You mean Eliza Gold and Constance Kent?'

'That's right. Did you know them?'

19

The Red Silhouette

THEY PEPPERED THE YOUNG SHEPHERD WITH QUESTIONS, and he was swift and sure of his replies. His speech was somewhat rough and not always coherent, but it came with such spontaneity and sincerity that the detectives could not help but believe him.

'The first time, he had another fellow with him, about the same age. People were always stopping in here back then, so I didn't pay much attention to begin with. But then he started smiling at Eliza – she was the one who served him, since she helped out in the pub most Saturdays – so I decided to keep an eye on him. And I noticed when he started whispering in her ear. The way she looked at him and nodded made me fear the worst. I stopped her to ask what he'd said, but she just brushed me off. I knew it then – the two of us were finished. She left a little before closing time, and who should go out after her less than a minute later? Nigel Manson. Of course, I didn't know his name then. Anyway, a few days later they fished Eliza out of the river. If she'd only stopped to think for a moment, she wouldn't have ended up like that.

'And then a year later, it happened again. Constance and I hadn't really spoken much, but I could tell she liked me. And I was in no rush – I had all the time in the world, or so I thought. Just like Eliza, Constance used to work Saturdays in the pub for a bit of extra money. When he walked in that evening, I recognised him right away. I'd only seen him once before, but I'll never forget his face. When Constance served him and he smiled at her, I knew what was going to happen. I was so angry, I stormed out of the pub right then. And they found Constance dead two days later. By then, I was very wary of this fellow, but I never saw him again… until last Saturday.'

'But what about the following year, when Annie Crook disappeared?' asked Hurst. 'Were you not in the pub that night?'

'I was, but I don't recall seeing him. Anyway, it was six or seven years ago now. And besides, I didn't have my eye on Annie the way I had with the other two.'

Hurst nodded, then asked, 'Why didn't you tell the police about this?'

'Well, they only started asking questions when Annie disappeared…'

'That's what I mean. They began to think there might be a mad sadist who dragged his victims up to Wish Tor…'

David Lynder finished his beer and slammed the empty tankard on the tabletop. 'I *did* tell the police. But they wouldn't listen. There were even a few people around here who suspected *me*. Can you believe that? And as for my story about the mystery man whose name I didn't know, and who nobody else remembered, and who I didn't even see on the night Annie went missing…'

'All right, I understand. Now, please tell us what happened last Saturday when you saw him again?'

The shepherd scowled. 'Well… naturally, it hit me pretty hard. I wanted to go over and punch him on the nose, but he was with Dr Grant and Basil and the professor, and they all seemed to be getting along well. I let him know what I think of him, though – I kept on staring, and I know he saw me. I doubt he would have remembered me, though.'

Hurst ordered another round of beers, then said casually,

'By the way, why were you out near Trerice Manor on Sunday afternoon, just before he died?'

David Lynder looked uneasy. 'I… I wanted to see him again. To talk to him, to… I knew who he was by then. That he was a great actor, or something. But I wasn't about to let that stop me.' He sighed wearily, then continued, 'I don't know if I would have had the courage after all. But I wanted to talk to him, and to… to…' He clenched his fists. 'To give him a beating he wouldn't soon forget!'

'We gathered that, yes. But what did you actually do?'

'Nothing. I had a look around the outside of the property, and then I heard a scream. I was too far away to see who it was lying on the ground, but somehow I knew it was him. So, I turned round and headed home. I still don't know if he was the one who murdered those girls, or if they drowned themselves because of him, but it doesn't matter. All I know is that the devil came back to claim one of his own.'

Minutes after finishing his story, David Lynder left the inn, but not before Hurst warned him not to stray far from the village for the time being. He lingered over by the bar for a minute or two before finally heading outside.

'I think our pleasant little chat has put a dampener on the rest of his evening,' said Hurst. 'Honestly, Twist, I could kick myself. We thought of every possibility except one: our phantom seducer was none other than Nigel Manson himself. It was so obvious… Now, I'm waiting for you to start casting doubts on the idea.'

Dr Twist polished the lenses of his *pince-nez* and said, 'Not at all, my friend. Not yet, anyway. He seemed genuinely sincere in his account and, of course, we know that Nigel Manson had a way with women. It's common knowledge that he was quite the lady-killer. We should have thought of it sooner – particularly when Mrs Manson told us outright that her husband had visited this remote part of the world before. She even said she suspected him of some sort of romantic dalliance out here. This fits perfectly with Mr Lynder's tale. While passing through Stapleford, the late actor had a tendency to court pretty young women.'

'Before throwing them off a cliff. Damn it all, this changes everything!' declared Hurst. 'So it was *him*, this sadistic demon of ours! And somebody worked it out and administered their own justice. I don't know about the invisibility business, but the rest is completely clear. You can imagine his surprise when Sitwell showed him a photograph of his three victims and told him the whole story. He seemed "intrigued" but really he was thinking of the best course of action so as not to give himself away! Which he must have done, one way or another. Someone in here realised he was the maniac who had wrought such havoc in the village all those years ago, and that same someone must have set in motion a diabolical plan to avenge those three young women. Nigel Manson had become an "invisible man," and so an invisible man would kill him. An eye for an eye, a tooth for a tooth. *That* is what went through the mind of our murderer.'

At that moment, Victor Sitwell entered the bar and Hurst repeated his deduction.

'So, all that remains,' the professor remarked, 'is to identify the culprit and the murder method.'

'Well, yes,' said Hurst with a slight grimace, 'but we're on the right track now. The culprit is evidently somebody from the village, who happened to be in the inn on Saturday night, and who's likely related to one of the victims. Well, Professor? Can you think of anyone who fits those criteria?'

'Difficult to say. A few names spring to mind, but I'm reluctant to pinpoint anyone specifically. Come to think of it, I doubt the photograph will be of much use to you now.'

'Indeed not,' said Hurst, 'because the murderer wasn't *in* the photograph – he was holding it!'

Sitwell nodded slowly. 'That strange expression as he looked at it. I mistook it for curiosity but, in fact, he must have been thinking hard, working out his next move.'

'But if you could let us see the photograph anyway,' said Twist gently, 'it would be much appreciated.'

'Gladly. You shall have it the day after tomorrow, as promised. And then I'll give it to George – I feel personally responsible for the stolen one. Ah, here's Basil…'

'Let's keep this between ourselves,' the inspector whispered to the professor. 'I don't have any suspects in mind at present, but better safe than sorry. The less warning our killer has, the better.'

Soon after Basil Hawkins' arrival the group was joined by Dr Thomas Grant. The beer flowed, and by ten o'clock the already flushed complexions of this merry band of drinkers had turned crimson. Basil went over to the bar to order another round, and while he was there he called for silence and then broke into a stirring rendition of *Rule Britannia*. Several other customers – some of whom were ex-Navy – joined in with gusto.

While they were catching their breath, Professor Sitwell commenced a speech on the merits of philanthropy.

'From a very young age,' he told them, 'I've always had a passion for equality. In fact, this almost led me to a political career. In Bodmin, which happens to be where I met Florence—'

'Funny,' put in Hurst, 'your wife mentioned that to us earlier, before you got home.'

'Yes, but that's another story altogether,' answered Sitwell, seizing his tankard of ale. 'Although it's related to everything else, of course, because if I hadn't met her at that point in my life, then I would likely have ended up following a very different path… which brings me back to my point. I was friends with several chaps who worked at the nearby tin mine. Conditions there weren't the worst, but they were nonetheless subjected to frequent indignities by the mine owner, who lived in a luxurious home nearby and regularly visited in his finest suit, driving his gleaming automobile – it was an outright provocation. So, I took matters into my own hands and organised several meetings with the miners. The following month, they went on strike. All of them, with a few rare exceptions. The owner flatly refused to countenance a wage increase, but the miners stood their ground. Can you guess what happened then? The coward chose to put a bullet in his brain rather than share his profits… but that's another story.

'It was then that I realised I had certain persuasive abilities, that perhaps I ought to embark on some sort of humanitarian mission… and that's when I met Florence.'

From there, the subject turned to the female of the species; the positives and negatives of married life, a subject which aroused feelings of nostalgia in Dr Grant. He said, not without humour, 'Don't talk about these things in front of an old bachelor like me, Victor. You ought to know better.' He looked around. 'Where's Basil? I didn't even see him get up…'

Frowning, Victor Sitwell peered round the room and said, 'I can't see him either…'

'I think *I* know what happened,' Hurst laughed drunkenly, 'he put on his magic ring and disappeared…'

By two o'clock in the morning, the little village of Stapleford was swathed in a heavy blanket of mist. A passer-by walking the streets would be scarcely able to make out a single light in the window of one of these dark buildings.

And yet there was such a light, and such a passer-by.

The lit window was that of Dr Twist's room, wherein the atmosphere was as dense and opaque as the fog outside. Sitting on his bed, propped up by a mound of cushions as he read through Professor Sitwell's notes, he puffed continuously on his pipe, pausing only infrequently to replenish his supply of tobacco. He concentrated intently on the pages, his darting eyes branding each word and sentence onto his memory. From time to time he glanced up at the ceiling, and nodded to himself with satisfaction.

As for the passer-by who walked the streets of Stapleford, it is rather difficult to paint any kind of portrait of this individual. A reddish silhouette moved very slowly through the fog, clearly anxious not to disturb the slumbering locals. But it paused for a moment beneath the lit window, and the yellow lamplight glinted briefly in a pair of eerily staring eyes, behind which lay a dark and unbalanced mind.

20

The Disappearance of Basil Hawkins

Dr Twist's face lit up as George Crawford served the two detectives' breakfast. Hurst smiled his thanks, and Twist pounced on a pile of golden toast.

'Quite foggy last night,' said the landlord. 'I think it's been giving my wife nightmares. She got up several times, and tells me she saw a figure in red prowling about in the street…'

'A figure in red?' asked Hurst.

'Someone in a red cloak with a hood. At least, that's what she says. But I ask you, who would be foolhardy enough to head out in a pea-souper like that? As far as I'm concerned, it was just part of her nightmare.'

'These things happen,' said Twist affably. 'Will you join us for a cup of tea, Mr Crawford?'

'With pleasure. In a moment, though; I have a couple of things I need to do first.'

When he was gone, Hurst asked Twist whether he'd found anything useful in the professor's notes.

'Absolutely, Archibald, absolutely. Professor Sitwell's account of the three tragedies is a veritable goldmine of information.'

'How so?'

'Well, nothing specific. It's more of an impression – a different viewpoint on the affair, packed with all the thousands of little details which paint such a distinct picture of village life. Every shade matters, and the background is constantly shifting.'

'I get the impression you don't plan on telling me anything useful.'

'And I, Archibald, get the impression that you got out of bed on the wrong side this morning. But it's an apt comparison, you know, between this case and a masterpiece...'

'Save it for your memoirs, Twist. All I'm interested in are the facts.'

'Well, I'm afraid there aren't any. Only a new impression, that's all. I'm quite sure that I have everything I need to solve the case... but I can't quite fit all the pieces together.' He rubbed his forehead. 'Do you understand? There are a few details I can't shake off. For instance, your idea of a long stick...'

'What? So, you reckon Nigel Manson was pushed from the window with a long stick after all?'

'You're putting words in my mouth, Hurst. I'm just trying to infer some sort of meaning from what you're saying. But there's no point, is there, since you're only interested in facts?'

Not for the first time, Hurst felt like taking his friend by the shoulders and shaking him. He resisted the urge on this occasion, though, and Twist slowly, delicately, sipped his tea, little finger in the air, apparently lapping up every last drop.

'However,' Twist continued, finally setting down his cup, 'there *are* a few observations I can share with you. We've overlooked certain obvious details, such as the fact that each of the three victims was working here at the inn on the night of their disappearance. And we can be fairly sure who it was that seduced those young women – but it's not quite enough. There's something else. Don't ask me what it is, though. I can't say for sure.'

Hurst put down his cup and favoured his friend with a smile much too pleasant to be the real thing. 'My dear Twist, not even the most cunning fox from some old fable could outsmart you. The wonderful detachment with which you deliver your mysterious pronouncements… but just because it amuses you, don't think I'm going to fall for it.'

'For heaven's sake, Archibald, I could swear you have some sort of persecution complex…'

'Every second we waste gives the killer further advantage, don't you agree? So, let's not waste any more time. Before we proceed, I think we need to briefly summarise this case – at least as far as the suspects are concerned.'

'An excellent idea. I'm listening.'

'We have a vague idea of the motive, but there remains the possibility of a crime of passion. So, let me classify our suspects in two distinct groups. The first group consists of the victim's wife, his mistress, her manager, or possibly some other individual yet to be identified; an acquaintance who has been careful to remain hidden. Here, the motive might be self-interest, hatred, jealousy, revenge, or something similar. At the top of that particular list I would place Helen Manson. She has the best motive by far. But, whilst the other two apparently have little motive to murder the actor, they seem more physically capable than Mrs Manson.'

'Quite right, Archibald. Although Miss Marvel is certainly charming, I'm sure she has the necessary willpower to kill. As does her manager; he has a certain quietude which makes for a formidable assassin.'

'Then we're agreed. Let's move on to the second group, which is much more populous. This is unfortunate, since it's fairly certain that our killer is lurking there. Indeed, it might be anyone in the village. There's no need to reiterate the motive; suffice it to say that our man discovered that Nigel Manson was responsible for the deaths of three young women, and so took his revenge. But who is he? Presumably someone who was here at the inn on Saturday night. I've just had an idea…'

'Yes?' asked Twist, busily scooping marmalade onto his toast.

'Well, couldn't it have been somebody who was sitting at the table with him? Wouldn't they be in the best position to see his reaction to the photograph?'

'Absolutely. I would also add the young shepherd, who by his own admission did not take his eyes off the actor as soon as he recognised him. Indeed, if you'll permit me a brief digression, he could very well have been entirely honest with us – told us the whole truth, only omitting the fact that it was he who committed the murder.'

'I think that's a bit of a stretch,' protested Hurst. 'Why would the murderer hand us the motive on a plate?'

'A double-bluff…'

'No, I really don't think he's intelligent enough for that sort of ruse. But I suppose you never know – often it's the opposite of our first impressions that turn out to be the truth. Let's move on to the others. Where shall we begin? Sitwell, Dr Grant, or Basil? Incidentally, speaking of Basil, I found his disappearing act last night rather curious…'

Dr Twist, who had devoured two slices of toast during Hurst's speech, thoughtfully smoothed his moustache. 'There's something peculiar about him, all right. He reminds me of somebody, but I can't recall who.'

'Can you see him in the role of a murderous vigilante?'

'No more than anybody else. But he's certainly not as naïve or gullible as he appears. And I'd be very careful not to judge him based on his penchant for liquor, which is no more prevalent among the weak-minded than it is among the intelligentsia. He has his share of secrets, I'd wager.'

'And Dr Grant?'

'He wouldn't hurt a fly. He's the very picture of kindness. But since we're dealing with vigilante justice, I suppose nothing is impossible. He seems to have a perfect alibi, just like everybody else, which isn't much use to us.'

'That leaves Sitwell.'

'I suppose the description of the doctor could also be applied to him. He's a man of integrity, and I doubt he would hesitate to…' Twist trailed off as the landlord returned to join them.

Once he was settled at the table, he talked about the weather, the village, the inn, before finally turning to the subject of the greatest tragedy of his life.

'They didn't find her body, but we didn't really expect them to. Our little Annie… she was only sixteen. Poor child… I'll never forget her face when Victor brought her here one evening – she looked like a frightened deer. And then, bit by bit, she got to know us. Of course she always had her own personality, and she could be difficult at times…'

These sad memories were even more poignant coming from such a burly, broad-shouldered fellow. His eyes misted over as he spoke.

'We understand,' said Hurst gently. 'I'm sure this is painful for you, but we need to know everything about the night she disappeared.'

'Well, she was a very pretty girl, with long brown hair…'

'It seems that she had started to attract attention…'

'True,' the landlord nodded gravely. 'For a few days before she went missing, she'd been acting differently. In a good mood all the time, humming to herself first thing in the morning… I assumed she had a boyfriend, but we never found out who it was.'

'By the way, was Nigel Manson here at the inn the night she disappeared?'

'It's so long ago now… No, I just can't remember. Let me call my wife, she has a much better memory than me.'

Shortly, Alice Crawford joined them. She was a plump, kind-looking woman with an aged, careworn face.

'I know exactly who you mean,' she said. 'He was here last Saturday with another gentleman, and the doctor, the professor and Basil. The problem is, on that particular evening, I barely set foot in the bar... so really, I can't say for sure.'

Hurst then asked if she had any specific memories of the evenings when the other two young women disappeared.

'A few, because we spent a long time talking about it afterwards. But it was still such a long time ago. I can't tell you anything about Constance Kent, because I was ill in bed that day. But as for the other one, Eliza Gold – she was the first to go missing – Saturdays were always busy in those days. Business was better than it is now, and we often had guests spending the night. It took a great deal of work, and we had several horses to look after back then...'

She suddenly turned a blank stare towards the two detectives.

'What is it, madam?'

'That Nigel Manson... do you know, I'm starting to think he *was* here that night... in any case, there was somebody who looked rather like him...'

'So we've been led to believe. At least, we have another witness who identified him.'

'Then it must be him. He had a friend with him, I think. They must have been very young. I remember now, because the girls had an argument about them in the kitchen. Eliza slapped Annie, and when I asked her why she said to me "She shouldn't be hanging around with boys at her age". Eliza was three or four years older than Annie, you see. And when she said "boys" I knew just who she was talking about. I'd seen her laughing and joking with them but, of course, it's natural for young people to have a bit of fun. And this is a pub after all – we expect the barmaids to be friendly. But I thought what Eliza said was interesting, because it seemed to me that *she* was the one who was flirting with the two lads, so I took a closer look at them. That's probably why I remember his face. But it's funny, I didn't make the connection until you mentioned it just now.' Her eyes widened and she went on, 'So, you think it was Nigel Manson who…'

'Seduced and then murdered those girls,' Hurst concluded. 'Yes, we have every reason to believe so. But apparently somebody took it upon themselves to take the law into their own hands. It seems that his death was no accident, so we're now looking for anybody with sufficient motive.'

21

The Mist on the Moor

VICTOR SITWELL SLIPPED INTO HIS DRESSING GOWN. That morning, his mood matched the bleakness of the landscape beyond the window. Following the tantalising aroma of the cooked breakfast waiting for him in the kitchen, he paused in the hall – a letter had been slipped under the front door. He rubbed his eyes and glanced at the clock; it was too early for the postman.

He picked up the envelope. The only writing on its exterior was his name, penned in capital letters. There was no postmark. He opened it, unfolded the letter and scanned the few lines of prose.

Minutes later, he sat down at the breakfast table.

'You certainly took your time. I heard you get up a while ago.'

'Nothing to worry about – I just remembered something I need to prepare for school, that's all.'

Florence Sitwell poured the tea. 'You seem distracted. Is it to do with what you told me last night? About Basil?'

'No… But you're right, his behaviour was rather strange. He disappeared all of a sudden, without any of us noticing. And without a word, which is very unlike him…'

'Perhaps he was offended by all that talk of him being a drunkard.'

'I don't think so. And besides, he never usually bothers about that sort of talk. No, I think it was something else.'

'You also said the inspector and that friend of his had come up with a new theory.'

'Yes – but it's much more than just a theory.'

'Maybe that's what upset Basil?'

'No, they told us about it before he arrived.'

Florence's expression suddenly darkened. 'And what do you make of it, darling?'

'Do I think the actor murdered those three girls?'

'No – who do you think pushed him from the window?'

'Ah, I couldn't possibly speculate…'

Later that morning, Nathalie Marvel stood by the window from which Nigel Manson fell to his death. She watched Archibald Hurst and Dr Twist walk away along the drive before disappearing through the gate. They had spent only thirty minutes at the house, explaining some of the latest developments in the case and asking a few pointed questions.

Nathalie turned. Helen Manson sat in an armchair looking pale but altogether composed after her latest interrogation. Perhaps widowhood was starting to suit her? After all, what difference did the death of an unfaithful husband really make?

Frank sat beside her. He gave a rather strained smile.

The actress retreated to her room and lay down on the bed. Barely five minutes had passed before the door creaked open and in walked the impresario.

'I do wish you'd knock,' she said mechanically.

He came and sat beside her on the bed, lighting up a cigar and pluming smoke in her direction. She blew it back in annoyance.

'I think it's fair to say that Nigel used and abused his powers of seduction,' Frank commenced, 'that seems very possible, does it not? But the idea that he spent his youth as a homicidal maniac murdering every girl who succumbed to his charms… I find that rather more difficult to believe.'

Nathalie Marvel sat up, brushing back a lock of blonde hair that had fallen over her face. 'I hardly think you're in a position to pass judgement on others.'

'Quite right, my dear, but that's not the point. It's the "homicidal maniac" bit that bothers me. The inspector was very amenable, I thought, but you and Helen can expect a much more rigorous interrogation to come. They'll want to know if he was ever violent with you.'

'Oh, shut up.'

'You can't avoid the question forever.'

'I don't know why they bother asking any questions at all, since they're so certain of everything.'

'Well,' said the impresario, getting to his feet again, 'if you ever want to leave this place, you'll have to answer them.'

Nathalie's temper flared. 'The sooner we get out of here, the better. I'm sick of this godforsaken house, and that silly woman. Although she seems to be coming out of her shell a little…'

'And I get the impression it will be rather a long time before you feel like playing *The Invisible Man* again…'

'To hell with it. I'm never doing that play again.'

Frank Holloway left the room, but not before turning back to his protégée with a knowing smile. 'As soon as we get back, I'll come up with something new for you. Something that's never been seen before, something that will really shake up theatreland! You'll see, Nat. We'll go far, you and me.'

Back in the drawing room, Frank Holloway wandered over to the window, where he gazed out thoughtfully for a few moments before settling on the sofa opposite Helen Manson.

'The fog is lifting,' he said, toying with one of his signet rings. 'We should see the sun again soon.'

Helen glanced at him and smiled – probably for the first time since her husband's death. 'I admire you, Mr Holloway.'

The impresario looked startled. 'You surprise me, madam. I had thought…'

'I must admit that I've never had much inclination for… let's say your "type". But I think I was mistaken in my impression of you.'

Holloway smiled. 'It doesn't matter, Helen.'

Cheeks flushed, Helen continued, 'Since Nigel died, you've been effectively dividing your time between Miss Marvel and me. You've conducted yourself with exemplary tact and discretion to keep the peace between us, which hasn't always been easy. To be honest, I never would have expected it of you. You've been a great comfort to me at this difficult time.'

'What if I told you I did it because I wanted to?'

'I wouldn't quite believe you.'

The impresario smiled again. 'Very well. Then let's just say you were mistaken about me.'

Helen Manson smiled back – much more broadly than before. 'My God,' she said, 'I'm starting to feel like myself again, even after everything we've just heard. Can you believe Nigel was capable of that? I can't quite fathom it. I could easily believe he'd had a few dalliances with local girls, since I already had my suspicions about that, but the rest of it… what do you think? Do you really believe he murdered those three girls?'

'I think perhaps you are better equipped to answer that question than I am, Helen. But since you ask, no, I never detected the slightest hint of sadism or malice in him.'

'Neither did I. But am I really the best person to judge? We had a few decent weeks after our marriage, but then everything changed…'

'Don't think about it, Helen. It will only be more painful for you. You must look to the future now.'

But Helen Manson was no longer listening to him. She grabbed a silver lighter from the table and flicked it mechanically several times before finally striking a light. She stared at the flame without blinking, and said in a dull voice, 'Even if it's true, I still need to know how he was killed. And who killed him.'

The sun was setting as Victor Sitwell clambered down from the attic, closing the trapdoor behind him. The smock he wore was carpeted with dust, but he had finally found what he was looking for. It had not been easy: he'd searched every nook and cranny before finally unearthing the photograph amongst a pile of old newspapers. How had it got there? He would never know.

After changing out of the smock, he spent a few minutes studying the photograph. 'My God,' he said to himself, 'how people can change in the space of ten years...' Florence was still a pretty young thing, and he himself looked much more vibrant. Dr Grant – who was standing not too far away from Eliza Gold – did not yet have the sad, weary smile that was now his habitual expression. He was looking over at Constance Kent, who really was a beauty. George and his wife stood behind Annie Crook, who was still a shy teenager in those days. David Lynder was barely visible, leaning against an amusement stall in the background. As for Basil, he stood out in a borrowed suit that was several sizes too small for him.

As he stared at the photograph, Victor Sitwell was overcome by an indefinable sensation. There was something in the picture – something he perceived unconsciously, but which his brain refused to interpret. An anomaly so astonishing that his mind could not comprehend it. Yes, there was a disparity between this photograph and reality... but what was it?

He heard the front door creak open downstairs, and dashed to the wardrobe to retrieve the envelope which had arrived for him that morning. He slipped the photograph inside and replaced the envelope in the pocket of his sports jacket.

When Florence entered the drawing room, she found him engrossed in the newspaper.

'My God, it's nearly six!' she exclaimed, glancing at the clock. 'Amazing how time flies. It's always the same when I visit the vicar's wife – and to think I only went over there for tea…'

'Tea loosens tongues. Particularly when you're an old gossip like she is.'

'Oh, speak for yourself. By the way, has Basil turned up? He said he'd trim the hedges today, but they look the same.'

'Basil?' the professor repeated, as though roused from a daydream. 'No, he didn't come. I can't believe I forgot. What on earth can have happened to him?'

'Don't you find it strange?'

'Yes… it's the first time he's let us down.'

At that same moment, Dr Thomas Grant was examining David Lynder, who had come to him complaining of a severe pain in his wrist.

'Nothing serious,' said the old doctor. 'Just a sprain. I'm going to put a bandage round it, and you're not to use that hand for a while. How exactly did it happen?'

'I tripped over a rock. Landed badly, that's all.'

The doctor's eyes widened. 'Tripped…? You're sure you weren't pushed?'

'No… I would have told you that, Doctor.' After a silence, he added, 'By the way, do you know if the police are getting anywhere?'

'I think so, though they don't tend to share their secrets with mere mortals like me.'

'They spoke to me last night. Or rather, interrogated me.' David Lynder recounted last night's conversation while the doctor bandaged his injured wrist.

When he had finished, the doctor stood thoughtfully for a

moment before saying, 'Did you hear what they've been saying in the village today, David? Apparently Mrs Crawford saw a figure in red walking the streets last night.'

The shepherd's expression turned severe and he murmured, 'Yes, I heard about it. You don't think…'

The doctor nodded slowly, as though weighing his words before speaking. His face was only partially illuminated by the dim light of his desk lamp, but the look of fatigue and distress was plain to see. 'Perhaps the police are onto something after all. Perhaps the killer *is* someone from the village. We thought so at the time, didn't we? But they're wrong on another point: this creature is unlike anything they've ever dealt with before.'

The old doctor approached David Lynder, looming over him. 'You see, when those three girls disappeared, I felt the presence of something truly evil walking the streets of Stapleford. It was almost a physical sensation, David, like the electricity in the air when a storm is about to break. And for the last few days, I've had that same feeling again. That same sinister, demonic presence… *demonic*, do you understand? The red silhouette prowling the streets… can't you see that this satanic creature is walking among us again?'

The clock in Weston's office struck half-past five.

'It's Friday,' said the Chief Constable. 'You arrived here at midday on Wednesday. I must say, for two and a half days' work it's not bad! We may not have the killer, but at least we have the motive. But I can't get over it – Nigel Manson, the homicidal maniac? What a story! Can you imagine the headlines?'

'Don't say anything to the papers yet,' instructed Dr Twist. 'It's only a theory, after all.'

'A theory?' Hurst repeated. 'What do you mean? We've clearly established the motive for Nigel Manson's murder…'

'It's the best explanation we've managed to come up with so

far, but it's still just a theory. Not only do we not know the name of the murderer, we also don't know how he did it.'

Hurst's surprise turned to disquiet. 'Twist, what's the matter? You seem very pessimistic all of a sudden. We've been discussing this for two hours – I thought you agreed with the theory!'

'I never said that I agreed. Only that I didn't object. There is a difference, my dear Archibald.'

'What do *you* think, then?'

'Well, as I've already told you, we seem to be missing at least three-quarters of your proposed solution. And there are other aspects of the theory that bother me. For instance, if Nigel Manson really murdered those three girls, why should he return to the scene of the crime – let alone buy a mansion there? No matter which way I look at it, he would have to be truly mad to do something so absurd. Almost as if he wanted to be caught. It would be like a game of Russian roulette – only more dangerous.' Hurst remained silent. 'In the meantime,' Twist continued, 'I think we'd better be heading off. It'll be getting dark soon, and the fog is coming down again.'

'Yes, don't wait too long,' Weston agreed. 'Soon the moor will be completely impassable.'

22

The Invisible Man

CHIEF CONSTABLE WESTON'S PREDICTION PROVED ACCURATE: it took Hurst over two hours to drive back into Stapleford. By the time he parked up the Talbot, his forehead was stippling with anxious sweat. The journey was no less nerve-wracking for Twist either – though he sat in the passenger seat, he was nonetheless obliged to endure the distressing spectacle of his friend driving blind. Hurst's eyes bulged as he struggled to negotiate the dense fog, and he grumbled constantly, his hands tight round the steering wheel.

Fortunately, George Crawford had kept their dinner warm for them. Once their bellies were full and they had recovered from the ordeal, the two men headed into the bar for a *digestif.* They did not stay long, though, for there were no familiar faces in the pub that night.

At around half-past nine they went to Dr Twist's room to discuss the case in peace and quiet. Inspector Hurst settled in the room's only chair, while Dr Twist began to pace the worn-out carpet. He walked from door to window and back again, lost in thought. He was so deep in concentration that he forgot to light up his pipe, even though he clutched it in his left hand while his right hand toyed with a pipe cleaner. The minutes ticked by, and Hurst began to lose patience.

'For heaven's sake, Twist, stop pacing. You're making me dizzy.'

'I'm not pacing. I'm thinking.'

'About what? Come on, spill the beans. You've been pacing — sorry, *thinking* — for three hours and you haven't said a word. Why did you ask me in if you didn't want to discuss the case?'

'Archibald, you know full well that simply having you around helps me to concentrate at pivotal moments in an investigation. And this is certainly a pivotal moment.'

'All right,' the inspector conceded, feeling flattered in spite of himself. 'Now, perhaps you'd care to let me in on the big secret…?'

Twist continued to pace back and forth across the carpet with metronomic rhythm, his right hand still toying with the pipe cleaner.

'What do you want me to say, Archibald? I could tell you how we've barely managed to fit two pieces of this damned puzzle together. Or I could tell you how we thought we were getting somewhere thanks to some sort of specious reasoning, only to end up right back where we started. If we assume that Nigel Manson murdered those three girls, I simply cannot see why he would come back to Stapleford. I suppose there's that old adage about the killer returning to the scene of the crime… but that's hardly gospel. Well,' Twist added, with a deep sigh, 'I don't suppose it matters all that much. It's only a tiny part of the puzzle, after all.'

'So, you don't have the slightest inkling as to how the murders were committed, let alone who committed them?'

Twist sighed again. 'Well… there *is* an explanation, but it seems so bizarre that I hardly dare mention it to you. Now, don't get excited, Archibald — it's not about the invisibility trick. It's a false testimony given by one of our suspects — except the person in question had no reason to lie… Forget it, Archibald, I don't know what I'm talking about.'

There was another silence, broken only by the sound of

Twist's endless pacing. Finally, Hurst said, 'You know, I had an idea this morning while we were at Trerice Manor. Of course, it's not entirely "rational", but it fits the circumstances well enough. Particularly considering how superstitious the locals are. While we were talking to Frank Holloway, I kept thinking about that story of the magic ring that makes the wearer invisible. Have you noticed those two signet rings he always wears?'

Outside, the fog was thicker than ever. Spewing from the surface of the stream, it had settled over the village, choking the streets like smoke. Under the dark arch of a doorway, Basil Hawkins was on lookout. He could scarcely see a thing through that fog, but he knew he couldn't abandon his station. He was quite certain that something important was going to happen tonight, and he had a major role to play.

He kept his ears pricked and his eyes glued to the narrow path beyond the inn; the path to Wish Tor. The Red Lion had closed its doors a good half an hour ago, but fortunately Dr Twist's window upstairs was still lit, casting its glow down onto the path so he would see even the slightest movement among the shadows.

Of course, there *was* another path up to the Tor, but it ran alongside the stream, and in this fog it would be sheer folly for anyone to attempt it. The slightest misstep on the slippery stones would send an unwary traveller spilling into the water, where the density of the fog and the enveloping darkness would likely seal their fate.

He heard a noise. Footsteps, as he had predicted. They were quiet, but he'd been waiting for so long in near-perfect silence that even the tiniest sound caught his attention. The pace was unhurried; casual. But the occasional variations in rhythm suggested caution.

Basil sensed that the walker was heading his way. Any moment, the silhouette would emerge from the fog.

At first, all he saw was a dark shape amid all that cottony whiteness, but then it paused in the rectangle of light emitting from Twist's window. He saw then that it was red; the same red silhouette he had spotted last night.

Pausing at the foot of the path, the figure looked towards the window of Dr Twist's room. In addition to his remarkable hearing, Basil's keen eyesight had been honed by the lengthy watch. So, in that dim light, he recognised the figure's face.

'Impossible,' he said to himself, his back pressed against the wall. 'It's impossible. So I *wasn't* mistaken last night after all…'

'His signet rings, Archibald?' Twist repeated with some amusement. 'You think they're magic, do you? By your logic, wouldn't that mean he should be invisible all the time?'

Hurst shrugged irritably. 'Well, what do you expect? This mad blur of facts and legends and ghost stories is obviously getting to me. At this point, I could believe just about anything.'

'Forgive me, my friend. And rest assured, you're not the only one.' With that, Twist resumed his pacing. 'But damn it all, the answer *must* be within reach. I'm quite certain we have all the information we need. I've answered a few questions to my own satisfaction, but they don't seem to add up to anything. Perhaps some of the pieces belong to a different puzzle altogether, but I'm convinced we have the key right in front of us – the one detail that casts a sudden, blinding light on the whole thing. We just need a trigger – usually I rely on *you* to provide that trigger…'

'Oh, that's right. Blame me for your own cerebral shortcomings. And for the last time, will you *please* stop playing with that pipe cleaner!' The exasperated inspector lurched forward to try to seize the pipe cleaner in question – alas, he not only failed to grab his target, but tripped on the frayed carpet and fell flat on his face.

Twist almost burst out laughing, but stopped himself. A strange expression crossed his face. As the inspector scrabbled to his feet, Twist silenced him with an imperious wave of his hand. For the next few minutes Hurst tried and failed to speak, silenced each time by that same gesture. And all the while, Twist continued to pace feverishly about the room, his eyes half-closed, muttering to himself in an almost trancelike state, '…which means we have to consider the possibility… yes, it must be… but then, what about the headless horseman…? No, no, Archibald, don't say anything. Don't break my train of thought. Like Ariadne, I must seize the thread that leads to the truth… Yes! Of course! It coincided with the departure of the gypsies…'

Then he shouted, 'Eureka! I have it at last! It explains absolutely everything! Thanks to you, Archibald, I can finally see the answer to this remarkable puzzle.'

Hurst looked sceptical. 'Including the murder of Nigel Manson?'

'Of course! In fact, that was the simplest part of the whole business! I can't believe how foolish we were not to spot it immediately. It's so simple – a little trick that was over in a quarter of a second – and the young actor went tumbling to his death. I must confess, in my entire career I have never before encountered such a seemingly impossible mystery with such a childishly simple solution – and I mean that literally. A childish solution. To think I was almost caught out by such a simple trick… I'm ashamed of myself.'

Dr Twist continued to chastise himself, slamming his palm with his fist, and even going so far as to strike the wardrobe door. This behaviour was very unlike him. However, while the blow he landed on the wardrobe was comparatively weak, it coincided with the sudden, startling shatter of the bedroom window.

Hurst and Twist jumped, then stood staring open-mouthed at the broken pane and the glass debris littered across the carpet.

'And you say *I'm* the one with the rotten temper,' growled Hurst.

'Archibald, I couldn't have done that just by hitting the wardrobe.' Twist went over to the window and peered out, but could see nothing beyond the white wall of fog.

'You think it was a vandal? I can't see a stone or a brick anywhere…' He examined the broken glass.

Tired of arguing, Twist went over to the bed. He began running through some of the possibilities for this strange phenomenon, from temperature fluctuations to a defect in the glass. Ten long minutes later, he dropped to his hands and knees beside the bed and peered underneath it. He eventually emerged in weary triumph, brandishing a small round object.

'Here's your stone,' he declared, 'it rolled under the bed, that's all.'

'Looks to be wrapped in newspaper,' said Hurst. 'Must be a message…'

Twist unwrapped the stone and smoothed the paper flat across the floor. Then he turned it over.

At first, all Hurst could make out was the newsprint, but then Twist pointed to the centre of the page. 'There's something there,' he said. 'It's hard to make out because it's written in pencil, but there's definitely a message, written in great haste…'

Hurst knelt down to read:

WISH TOR, QUICKLY. THE DEMON IS LOOSE AGAIN.

'We don't have a moment to lose,' said Twist. 'Come on.'

'You want us to go up there now? In these treacherous conditions?' the inspector stammered.

'Someone is in grave danger, Archibald. And I'd hate to see

another victim killed just because I wasn't quick enough to solve the puzzle.'

Within five minutes, the two detectives were traversing the path up to Wish Tor. Hurst was doing his best to light the way, but the beam of his flashlight was swallowed up by the fog.

'This is dreadful,' he muttered, 'I can barely see six feet in front of me…'

They almost strayed from the path several times, but each time the unexpected appearance of ferns, heather and foliage beneath their trampling boots alerted them.

Then the slope grew steeper. They were halfway up the tor when the silence was shattered by a distant scream. It was short, but evidently a scream of absolute terror.

The two detectives froze, looking at each other.

'What was that?' the policeman asked.

'I fear the worst, Archibald. Come on, there isn't a moment to waste.'

They resumed their uphill trudge, picking up speed, but lost their way once again, taking a path to the right which started to lead them downhill once more. Realising their mistake, they turned back when they suddenly heard the sound of hurried footsteps.

'Someone's running downhill,' the inspector growled, peering into the fog. 'Who is it? I can't see a damn thing. What shall we do, Twist? Go after him?'

'It would be pointless, he's got such a head start. I can hardly hear him now, he's almost gone. Come on, let's get back on track.'

Eventually, they reached the summit of Wish Tor. The fog had not abated, but there were occasional patches where it seemed to thin out, revealing the looming shadow of rocks here and there. It was in one of these thinner patches that they glimpsed the plateau up ahead.

Hurst pointed, crying out, 'Over there! Look, there's someone there!'

'You're right. It looks like a woman…'

There was indeed a female figure wandering ahead of them. At first, she seemed to be looking for the path, but then changed her mind. In fact, her behaviour was quite bizarre: she paced back and forth, and seemed to be speaking to someone.

'Twist!' the inspector whispered. 'Tell me I'm dreaming! That's Nathalie Marvel, isn't it?'

'I believe it is.'

'And it looks as though she's talking to someone… someone we can't see…'

Short of breath but with a keen eye, Twist surveyed the scene like a bloodhound, before tugging at his friend's arm.

'We need to get closer. Turn off your flashlight.'

With the utmost care, they climbed the remaining distance to the plateau. As they approached, they heard snatches of conversation. Soon enough, they distinctly made out Nathalie Marvel's voice. She spoke cheerfully, playfully, but her amusement seemed to be giving way to irritation.

'Yes, yes, all right,' she said, 'but really, I must go now. I'll catch pneumonia if I stay up here much longer. I shall think about what you've said. But honestly, you could have chosen a better spot to confess your feelings…'

Twist and Hurst were now close enough to perceive the scene with relative clarity. Concealing themselves behind a large rock, they watched as the actress inched dangerously close to the edge of the cliff, silhouetted against a backdrop of swirling, milky fog and jagged rocks. But there was nobody with her.

'Shouldn't we do something?' whispered the inspector.

'Wait a moment.'

Suddenly, Miss Marvel flinched, and her voice rose sharply. 'That's enough, Professor! Don't touch me again. If your wife knew what you were up to… wait, what are you doing? Let go of me! You're mad! No!'

The detectives sprang from their hiding place, but it was too late. The actress had vanished over the edge.

23

Over the Edge

Horrified, the two men stared at the spot from which Miss Marvel had just fallen. A few feet away from them, the edge of the cliff was swallowed by dense, swirling fog.

'It's not possible…' Twist said softly, 'I don't understand…'

'But… we saw him with our own eyes!'

'Who?'

'Whoever it was! The invisible man!'

'We saw the invisible man with our own eyes,' deadpanned Twist.

'This is no time for sarcasm, Twist. If you'd listened to me, we might have been able to prevent this. When I think of that speech of yours earlier… well, we've got to face facts now. And to think I wasted so much time on your ridiculous theories!'

'Careful now, Archibald,' said Twist, 'don't say anything you're likely to regret.'

The inspector shrugged and then, in a calmer, more contrite tone, said, 'Well, now we know the name of the monster. I must admit, Victor Sitwell was hardly at the top of my list. How about you?' Twist did not reply. 'All right, come on. Let's get out of here. He can't be far away. He's probably listening to us somewhere right now…'

Strangely enough, Twist did not follow his friend's advice. Instead of withdrawing, he stepped towards the edge of the cliff. Peering over, he cried out, 'Archibald, look! We're not directly over the water. There may yet be a chance… Quick, hand me your flashlight!'

He swept its beam along the rough, rocky face of the Tor. In places, the slope was not quite so steep, and extended out into wide ledges like the side of a pyramid. It was on one of these ledges, some fifty feet below, that a body lay unmoving.

'It's her!' exclaimed Twist. 'And there might still be a chance…'

Swiftly, the two men descended the slope, reaching Nathalie Marvel in less than a minute.

As Twist took her pulse, Hurst stared in horror at her fingertips. They were bloodied from her desperate attempts to cling to the rocks as she fell. Her face was virtually unmarked – the only visible injuries were a couple of grazes on her cheek and forehead.

'She's alive,' Twist announced.

'Thank God for that…'

'A broken leg, I think,' observed Twist, 'maybe a few other fractures. All the same, she's been incredibly lucky.'

'You can say that again! This fog was a stroke of luck, too – otherwise the murderer might have finished her off.'

Twist turned to his friend, who was still studying the actress's beautiful (albeit bruised) face, framed by the silky blonde curls and the hood of her red cloak. 'That would have been dreadful, wouldn't it?' Twist remarked.

Suddenly, her lips parted. She drew a sharp breath, and her long, dark lashes fluttered open. She peered around. 'Where am I? What happened? Oh, God, my leg…'

'No need to be frightened now, Miss Marvel,' Hurst told her gently. 'We're here. You're safe.'

'In a way, perhaps,' Twist cut in. 'But let me tell you something, Annie Crook: this grotesque charade won't save you from the gallows. Not even those fluttering eyelashes of yours can do that. Take a good look at that face, Archibald. She's no angel.

She is a monster. A demon. She's responsible for the murders of Eliza Gold, Constance Kent, Nigel Manson and, I fear, Victor Sitwell.'

24

The Art of Deduction

'So you want to tell us the whole story now, Twist? Surely that's too easy now that she's confessed?' said Hurst wryly, before taking a sip of sherry. He continued, 'Of course, I wouldn't dream of depriving you of your big moment. These denouements are a speciality of yours, after all.'

It was now a whole week since the death of Nigel Manson, and it was at the very scene of the tragedy that Dr Twist was about to reveal the truth behind the mystery to Helen Manson and Frank Holloway, as well as Dr Thomas Grant, who had been invited for the occasion, and Basil Hawkins – though he was already apprised of part of the story. As for Victor Sitwell, he had been in a hospital ward in Tavistock since the early hours of Saturday morning. His condition wasn't serious; there was even talk of sending him home the next day.

Dusk had descended on this rainy Sunday in late August. There was a peculiar atmosphere in the drawing room – a sense of feverish anticipation with which Hurst was all too familiar. The others were hanging on Twist's every word.

He waited a moment before responding to his friend's somewhat acidic remark. 'Archibald, you know full well that I worked out the whole thing on Friday evening. Thanks to you, by the way.'

'How would I know that, since you refused to share even the tiniest bit of your theory?'

'All right then. In that case, we must let our audience be the sole judge of my detective work. I realise now that "the whole story" is perhaps rather ambitious, since it would have been impossible to work out why Annie Crook – alias Nathalie Marvel – went over the edge of the cliff that night. But we know now, thanks to her confession. Incidentally, she fainted when they told her they couldn't save her leg, and that she could kiss her acting career goodbye…'

'A curious reaction,' said Hurst, 'for someone who knew well enough that she was headed for the gallows.'

'Personally, I think it fits very neatly with her psychological make-up. But let's get back to this notion of "the whole story". Really, it's the only possible solution to be derived from a careful sifting of the facts, combined with a hint of common sense and a smattering of imagination. The turning point came when I realised with absolute certainty that only Nathalie Marvel could have murdered Nigel Manson. It was an astonishingly simple murder, in spite of the apparent impossibility which gave it a supernatural flavour. Incidentally, the solution presented itself to me thanks to a rather amusing incident involving my friend Hurst, but we can return to that specific point later. I was already suspicious of Nathalie Marvel because she told us two blatant lies.

'To the untrained observer, the first lie might not seem obvious because it's based on a certain behavioural quirk. But to a psychologist, it's very telling. We asked Nathalie Marvel about what she saw, or could have seen, in the seconds preceding Nigel Manson's fall. Remember, she had him in the camera's viewfinder. Had she seen anything on the roof, or in one of the adjacent windows? She thought carefully, then answered no. But you see, she *thought carefully.* It was as if she were sifting through her memories to recall the scene. And yet, she was photographing Nigel Manson at the moment he fell – and the camera only affords a very narrow field of vision, as that last picture demonstrates. You can't see anything but the actor and the window frame. There's no way she could have spotted anything beyond that, and she wouldn't need to think about it before saying so. All she could see through the viewfinder was the actor sitting on the window sill.

'As a consummate actress, she was playing the role of an innocent photographer. That's the impression she wanted to give. Since we knew from witnesses that she really *was* photographing Nigel Manson seconds before the tragedy, we must wonder what this strange behaviour means. She wanted us to believe she was photographing Nigel Manson, when she really *was* photographing him. Unless, perhaps, she wasn't? Unless, for a split second, she actually did something else?

'Her second lie is less subtle, but she pulled it off brilliantly. It pertains to your return from the inn on Saturday night, Mr Holloway. Nathalie Marvel stated that Nigel burst into her room in the middle of the night after mistaking it for his own, and that she immediately threw him out. You, Mr Holloway, told us something completely different; you claimed that you saw Nigel Manson in Nathalie Marvel's room, and that the two of them were talking in hushed tones for quite some time. A blatant contradiction. When our investigation forced us to question it, she skilfully parried the blow by implying that Nigel Manson had burst into her room and made a drunken pass at her, which she had tried to keep quiet for obvious reasons…

'This was doubly clever, because decency prevented us from dwelling further on the matter. And so she succeeded in deceiving us about the nature of her conversation with Nigel Manson that night, which had actually gone on for much longer than she first claimed and which, as we shall see, was considerably more significant than she let on.

'Those were her two lies. But at that stage, the case was still too tangled for me to draw an effective conclusion. However, my absolute certainty that she was responsible for the murder prompted me to search for a link between this crime and the three others – the fate of those unfortunate girls from the village. And this led me to uncover her real identity.

'It was quite a dilemma, since the various witness testimonies pertaining to those three incidents seemed to preclude any kind of rational explanation. First, we have the headless horseman, witnessed by our friend Basil, which then took flight and soared off into the night sky. A drunken stupor? Possibly. And yet, I was convinced there must be at least a grain of truth in it.

'Then we have John and Betty's account of the death of Constance Kent. Disturbing, certainly, but not inexplicable. What exactly had they seen? A girl walking towards them alone, looking for somebody and calling out to them, before stopping at the edge of the cliff. Nothing particularly out of the ordinary there. She behaved as though she was expecting to find somebody waiting for her, but the person had not appeared.

'Now, let us imagine that this other person *was* there, that she had, in fact, hidden herself behind a rock before the young lovers arrived. This would be quite easy to do, as Hurst and I found out for ourselves. And let us imagine that she had gone there with the express purpose of murdering Constance Kent. Was she going to let these two interlopers spoil her plan? Certainly not. She had more than one trick up her sleeve. When the time came, all she had to do was reach out from her hiding place with a long stick and simply poke Constance in the back, causing her to fall. Don't forget, it was the dead of night; the darkness worked in her favour.'

'Don't tell me,' Frank Holloway interrupted, 'that she killed Nigel that way too?'

'No, Mr Holloway, certainly not. Nor was Madeleine Hall killed that way either. But is it written anywhere that each crime must be committed in exactly the same way? No. Furthermore, Professor Sitwell's excellent notes informed me that, during the search he undertook with Dr Grant and Basil the following morning, they didn't find anything in the water at the foot of Wish Tor – except for a wooden stick.

'The only other information pertaining to Constance Kent's disappearance came from Annie Crook – and it came rather late, too; she didn't share her story until after the police became involved. And what she had to say was truly incredible. She claimed that she saw Constance Kent from her bedroom window at about eleven o'clock, and that Constance was walking away from the inn and chatting to a person who wasn't there. This is downright impossible, whichever way you look at it.

'But then, this account was supported by Basil's testimony the following year, when he saw Annie Crook herself heading towards Wish Tor with another invisible companion who was just as cheerful as the previous one...'

Basil folded his arms with a hint of a smile.

'That was another Saturday night,' Twist continued, 'so it's not surprising that our friend's faculties were somewhat... impaired. But still, one can't use drunkenness to rule out his testimony every single time. Generally speaking, I tend to think that excessive alcohol is a convenient excuse... but enough of that. The important fact here is that the most extraordinary aspects of these two disappearances rely in some capacity on Annie Crook. In the first, she was the witness, and in the second she was the leading lady.

'So you see, if we conclude that Annie Crook is a liar then most of the mystery is explained. In fact, all that's left is the matter of the headless horseman. The trick is that Annie Crook was always believed to be one of the victims... and yet, wasn't she the only one whose body was never found? The circumstances of her disappearance left little doubt that she had met the same fate as the other girls. And yet, as my friend Hurst can attest, in cases like this, it doesn't do to trust in corpses that are never found.

'That was the conclusion I had reached about the three disappearances. I therefore settled on the idea that Annie Crook might be the murderer, though I had no idea of the motive. But my absolute certainty that Nathalie Marvel killed Nigel Manson, coupled with my theory that the same assassin was responsible for both this crime and the prior disappearances, caused me to wonder if she and Annie Crook might be the same person. So, I thought about their ages: Annie Crook was sixteen when she disappeared, and that was seven years ago… therefore, she would be exactly the same age as Nathalie Marvel. Nathalie was blonde, and Annie Crook wasn't? No matter: Nathalie's hair was dyed.

'Next, I looked into Nathalie Marvel's past – of which very little was known, except for what you, Mr Holloway, told me. You said she was an acrobat in a circus when you met her. A circus? It would be rare to find a circus that didn't feature at least one or two gypsies, particularly those who are acrobats or particularly good with horses… And that's when I remembered another detail from Victor Sitwell's notes: there were gypsies in Stapleford when Annie Crook disappeared, and they left the village the very next day.'

'The way you explain it, it all seems crystal clear,' commented Frank Holloway with an admiring nod.

'I told you,' said Hurst, 'my friend is quite the storyteller.'

'That last point,' continued Twist imperturbably, 'was doubly revealing. Not only did it support my theory that Nathalie Marvel was really Annie Crook, but it also supplied an excellent clue to the murderer's psychology. Abandoning the security of home for a new life travelling the country in a caravan denotes a certain strength of character, a need for change, and perhaps also a sense of disgust with one's past. In other words, a fiercely independent adventurer.'

'A certain strength of character…' repeated the impresario with a distant look. 'Now there's an understatement. I've never met a girl as determined as she is. Once she's decided on something, there's nothing anyone can do to stop her.'

'My point exactly, Mr Holloway. But first, let's move forward in time to her first meeting with Nigel Manson. You were there too, of course. It provides us with another invaluable clue to the motive for those first two murders. You told me that you've never encountered such an obvious instance of love at first sight. More specifically, that you've never seen such lust in a woman's eyes. What does this tell us, bearing in mind that Annie Crook had met Nigel Manson before, at the inn? Surely, if a person becomes suddenly infatuated with somebody they have already met, it's because they have been carrying a torch for them for a long, long time?

'Therein lies the root of evil. Lust is one of the most powerful forces on the planet, and it's also the cause of countless tragedies. This is nothing new, of course, but it's still troubling to see that the cycle repeats itself so predictably. Annie's adoptive mother, Mrs Crawford, recalled one last detail which is vital to the solution. On the night she disappeared, Eliza Gold slapped Annie and told her to stop bothering one of the young men in the bar. That young man, we now know, was Nigel Manson.

'Did Annie Crook see herself as Eliza's love rival, though she was only sixteen years old? It might seem shocking, but it's really not all that unusual for a girl of that age to take a fancy to a handsome stranger. Eliza's slap – a brutal humiliation – followed by the insult of Eliza's own flirtation with Nigel Manson, provoked a sudden rage in Annie Crook. This was compounded by the sight of her "Prince Charming" whispering sweet nothings in Eliza's ear before the two of them slipped out of the pub later that night.

'Victor Sitwell's notes told me that one of Annie Crook's duties at the time was to take care of the stables. Taking her favourite horse and galloping out across the moor – surely a perfect outlet for an adolescent with a broken heart? Naturally, and that's exactly what Annie did. And while she was out riding, she glimpsed in the moonlight Eliza's silhouette on the top of Wish Tor. She was alone. Now, it might seem unusual for a girl to remain up there after her suitor has departed, but let's not forget how the tor got its name: it is supposedly a place that grants wishes. So perhaps that is what Eliza was doing up there – making a wish following her dalliance with Nigel Manson.

'Either way, young Annie's rage returned, and she set the horse off galloping up the slope towards the rocky outcrop. She raised the collar of her cloak above her head, to impersonate the fabled headless horseman in the hopes of giving Eliza a much-deserved scare.

'Was it fear that caused Eliza to fall from the edge of the cliff and down into the water? Or was she pushed deliberately? Now, of course, Annie is sticking to the former version of events. But we only have her word for it.'

'So, that was it,' said Holloway. 'The headless horseman, riding off into the sky.'

'I must have been fairly far-gone not to see that she was galloping up Wish Tor,' said Basil. 'But still, it's nice to know that my eyes weren't deceiving me. I really did see a headless horseman riding off into the sky.'

'In any case,' Twist continued, 'that was the source of all the rumours. And when a deck of cards was found in Eliza Gold's pocket – hardly unusual, since she'd spent the evening at the inn which was packed with drinkers who liked to gamble – it nonetheless called to mind the legend of Jan Reynolds, who was carried away to hell by the devil, and who dropped a deck of cards as he went. The "obvious" conclusion was that Satan himself had come for Eliza Gold.

'And that was the end of it – until the following year, when the scenario repeated itself. Nigel Manson was passing through the village again, and happened to stop at the inn. This time, though, he set his sights on Constance Kent. David Lynder, the young shepherd, saw the two of them flirting. And as for Annie Crook, we don't know exactly what she did that evening, but it's not too difficult to imagine: her handsome Prince Charming has returned – but he leaves with another girl once again. And so Constance Kent's fate is sealed.

'As for how Annie lured Constance up to Wish Tor, I can only speculate, but it seems that a forged letter from her suitor might do the trick. Anyway, we know the rest: a gentle nudge from a stick concealed behind a rock… and Constance takes the plunge.

'Let me remind you that Annie had no intention of pinning the crime on an "invisible man" – it came about simply so that John and Betty did not see her. And since the villagers had characterised her last crime as the work of the devil, she decided to lend credence to that theory by scattering a deck of cards in the field beside the stream.

'When John and Betty's statement provoked rumours of an invisible killer, Annie didn't hesitate. Police questioned her and she swiftly invented a sighting of Constance Kent chatting to an invisible man en route up to Wish Tor. I get the impression that she was conflating two local legends here: the abduction of Jan Reynolds by the devil and the tale of the invisible man who pushed a witch to her doom. Not that it mattered, of course; not a single person in the village doubted her claim.

'And the following year she arranged her own "disappearance". It didn't take much: just a bit of lovestruck playacting, and finding a witness to see her talking to the invisible man before disappearing forever with the gypsies.

'The only question that remains is *why* she had to disappear. There are probably several reasons, and our understanding of her psychology is useful: her ambition, her inability to remain in one place, her dull existence in Stapleford. Perhaps even remorse, and the desire to escape the scene of her crimes.

'As for the spectacular nature of her disappearance, and the return of the mysterious "demon-lover" – let's not forget that we're dealing with an actress. Running away would not be enough for Annie Crook – she needed to stage something spectacular, to completely sever all ties to her previous life.

'Well, I think that effectively concludes the first act of this tragedy, so I suggest we move on to the second act without further ado. You'll soon see that Nathalie Marvel had no recourse but to kill again in order to save her own skin. You will also learn how she murdered Nigel Manson. This murder was, if you'll forgive the expression, a genuine marvel – from a purely aesthetic point of view.'

25

A Genuine Marvel

Dr Twist removed his *pince-nez* and turned his sympathetic gaze towards Helen Manson. She remained utterly composed. 'I understand that this is very painful to discuss, but I'm afraid for the sake of clarity it must be said.'

'I'm not the grieving widow you think I am, Dr Twist,' she answered, meeting his gaze. 'Time and the truth have done their work.'

'I'm glad to hear it, madam. Then let us return to Miss Marvel's infamous lust for Nigel Manson. Incidentally, I ought to point out that, while it's perfectly natural for her to recognise her "Prince Charming" right away, it's equally natural that he made no connection between this vivacious blonde and the young girl from Stapleford. After all, he had paid little attention to her at the time, reserving his attention for Eliza Gold and Constance Kent, two girls of his own age.

'You know the old saying, "what a woman wants…" Well, it was never more accurate. What Nathalie Marvel wanted, she got. And in this case, it was Nigel Manson. But as the months passed, and her fame grew thanks to the play's undeniable success, perhaps she began to realise that her "Prince Charming" wasn't so charming after all, and that he was no more of a prince than anybody else. Don't misunderstand me: she still harboured feelings for him, but he was no longer the object of her obsession. That was now her acting career. Which explains

160

why she didn't hesitate to kill him when she had to. In light of what we now know, it's not difficult to imagine the shock she received about ten days ago when a telegram arrived from Nigel Manson, inviting both herself and you, Mr Holloway, to spend the weekend in Stapleford of all places…'

'Where she might be recognised at any moment,' put in Frank Holloway. 'I see now why she was so against the idea, and why she came up with all those excuses to try to get out of it. At the time I found it rather strange.'

'However,' Twist continued, 'once the initial moment of panic passed, she decided to go along with it. After all, she was quite convinced that an actress of her calibre would have no trouble finding convincing excuses not to step outside the house for two or three days. Of course that's why she categorically refused to spend an evening at the inn, even though it meant being left alone with her romantic rival. But this is where her trouble began. At around two o'clock in the morning, Nigel Manson came to her room, waking her with news of a strange photograph…

'Here, we must leap from the mind of the killer to that of the victim. What must have gone through his mind when he saw that photograph, and learned the fate of those three young women? Of course he recognised Eliza Gold and Constance Kent – and then he learned that they were both murdered, the dates corresponding exactly to the nights he met them. He didn't say a word about this at the inn, no doubt fearful that it might damage his reputation. Even if he *had* felt like discussing it further, he changed his mind as soon as he learned that both girls were killed so soon after he had been with them. The third girl, Annie Crook, didn't ring a bell. But then, gradually, he began to realise…'

'That she was Nathalie Marvel,' suggested Helen.

'Well, at the very least, he must have noticed the resemblance. But he was drunk, and not thinking straight. He spent a long time staring at that photograph during the evening. What was going through his mind? Two of those young women were former lovers of his, and the third resembled his current mistress. Quite a coincidence.

'Now, I had the opportunity to see this infamous photograph when we found a copy on Nathalie Marvel after her sojourn up to Wish Tor. It's not a perfect shot, but the most remarkable aspect is how clearly the face of Annie Crook stands out from the crowd. Since Nigel Manson had plenty of opportunity to observe Miss Marvel up close, I've no doubt that he noticed the striking resemblance.

'But what did he deduce from that resemblance? We can't know for sure. Did he work out that Annie Crook had murdered the other two girls? Somehow I doubt it. Either way, he signed his own death warrant by visiting his mistress in the dead of night to ask her about it – particularly since he had invited some villagers to visit him at the mansion the following day.

'Naturally, she knew there would be dire consequences if anyone recognised her. The miraculous resurrection of Annie Crook was bound to cause shock waves – even the best possible outcome would seriously harm her career. Of course, she *could* try running away again – though this would not alleviate the danger posed by Nigel. He might mention the "resemblance" to anyone; indeed he was likely to bring it up as a topic of conversation the following afternoon. "And may I present the famous Miss Nathalie Marvel – isn't she a dead ringer for the late Annie Crook?"

'She needed to get rid of him, that much was certain. He was no longer her "Prince Charming", but a troublesome encumbrance. Oh! I nearly forgot – obviously it was Nathalie Marvel who stole the photograph from the inn. She sneaked over there after Nigel went to bed.'

'But,' Dr Grant interrupted, 'how did she get in…?'

'You forget, sir,' smiled Twist, 'that she had lived there for several years.'

'Of course,' Grant shook his head ruefully, 'stupid of me. But I still can't quite comprehend it… that little girl…'

'Well, this was the problem that presented itself to Nathalie Marvel. But she was quite confident that her blonde hair, fuller figure and her invaluable sunglasses could fool the villagers… at least for a little while. It's no coincidence that she was outside during the afternoon, pretending to photograph the garden…'

Twist fell silent for a moment.

'You're probably wondering,' he resumed, 'how she managed to murder Nigel Manson whilst she was taking a photograph of him in the upstairs window, as confirmed by Professor Sitwell. Well, as I said, it's absurdly simple, and would take no more than a second…'

With that, Twist stared down at the empty glass in his hand, then suddenly lobbed it towards Frank Holloway. It was a rather weak throw, and the glass fell three or four feet in front of him. Nonetheless, Holloway caught it, springing reflexively from his seat and landing on his knees.

'Do you see now?' Twist asked quietly. 'Throw a precious object towards somebody sitting on a window sill, slightly out of reach… the other individual's instinct is to reach forward and catch it. It's so simple, and it works every time. But please… I urge you not to try it at home.

'Nigel Manson treasured his cameras as though they were his children – that was well-known. And Nathalie also knew there was a good chance that if she offered to take his photograph he might spring into one of his trademark acrobatic poses.'

'He had his arms stretched out…' murmured Helen Manson. 'My God.'

'Yes, he was trying to catch that precious camera. It was a simple reflex, but from inside the house it looked as though he'd been pushed. But let's not forget the context for the crime: the play of *The Invisible Man* and, of course, the tragic events which took place in this house half a century ago. To the casual observer, the real-life "invisible man" was back.

'All the same, Nathalie Marvel was very, very lucky. Not with her throw – she was a trained acrobat, after all, and obviously highly skilled at timing a throw – but with the arrival of Professor Sitwell. She didn't know he was there, of course – he was walking across the lawn, so she couldn't hear his footsteps. But she was lucky because he had her in his line of sight the entire time – except when he passed the rhododendron bushes. In his very detailed account, the professor said he could see the victim at the moment he fell – directly above a bush. In other words, he couldn't see what was happening on the ground at that moment.'

'Even if he *had* seen her,' commented Frank Holloway, 'she could have played it off as a practical joke – albeit with a tragic outcome.'

'Good point, Mr Holloway. And I'm sure Nathalie Marvel had thought of that. If caught in the act, all she would have to do was say (amid much fluttering of eyelashes) "I only wanted to play a little trick on him…" That's why I still think it was a clever murder in many ways. Of course, she couldn't have known for sure that the fall would kill him, but there was a good chance it would leave him seriously injured, which would temporarily avert the danger he presented. And then she could have finished him off at her leisure.'

'By the way,' said Holloway, 'you haven't told us about Madeleine Hall's death. Was that another murder using the same method?'

'Well, we may never know for sure, but personally, my answer is yes. In some ways – and do forgive me, Mrs Manson – that long-ago crime is even more sinister than the one we've just been talking about. You see, in this instance, the culprit was a child – Madeleine's stepdaughter, Celia.

'From the bottom of the stairs, she threw her doll – all wrapped up in a blanket – towards her new stepmother. She must have truly hated her, likely resenting her for usurping her mother's place, but also because Madeleine seemed to neglect her in favour of the baby. You can probably guess what the doll in a blanket looked like to Madeleine Hall on that ill-lit landing. If you'll forgive me for dwelling on the morbid details of this case, I suggest that you imagine yourself in Madeleine's place. You are a mother or father at the top of that dark staircase… you see a figure at the bottom of the stairs, cradling something which looks like a tiny infant swathed in a blanket and then… from nowhere, it comes flying up towards you!

'Sir Edward must have realised what had happened. The fact he became a recluse after his second wife's death implies that he had overwhelming feelings of guilt about something. And, since we'll never know for sure, I don't mind speculating that it was Celia who planted the ring. She presumably knew the story of Vixina the Witch, who was vanquished by an invisible man with a magic ring – and she was also keen to paint Madeleine as a witch. But her father didn't fall for it, and that's why he came up with that rather feeble excuse for the ring's presence at the top of the stairs.'

'I'm starting to think you're a bit of a sorcerer yourself,' said Dr Grant, and it was not immediately clear whether he was joking. 'You've explained away every part of the mystery like magic. Well, almost every part. How did Nathalie Marvel end up using exactly the same murder method as the one from fifty years ago?'

Dr Twist took his time in answering. 'Well, Nathalie Marvel claims the murder of Nigel Manson wasn't premeditated. She says she was walking the garden in desperation, camera in hand,

and that the idea of killing Nigel – at least, the method for killing him – came to her at the very moment she took that photograph. Supposedly, the situation reminded her of an accident she saw during a performance by a juggler in the circus. Personally, I don't believe it – the fact that she had the camera in her hand seems a little too convenient. But I *do* believe she saw that accident. In fact, I think it was the memory of that accident that enabled her to unravel the mystery of Madeleine Hall's death, which Nigel Manson had told her about. This story, as well as her two previous crimes, began to blend in her imagination when the actor was foolish enough to mention the photograph to her the previous night.

'Oh – I almost forgot another clue. Not a vital clue, admittedly, but a useful one: the camera, which she claimed to have dropped in shock at the sight of Nigel's fall, was shattered into "a thousand pieces". That's how Colonel Weston described it. Rather curious, you might think, if it had only fallen a few feet.

'Which leaves us with one last question: the draught of air that immediately preceded your husband's fall, Mrs Manson. Personally, I think it was just an ordinary draught that arises when a door opens. What do you think, Mr Holloway?'

The impresario smiled like a gambler realising just too late that he has a losing hand. 'I know,' he said, 'it was a foolish lie on my part, particularly since it was so unnecessary. As you already worked out, I heard Nigel calling to Nathalie because my bedroom window was open. When I saw him sitting in the window with Nathalie on the ground below, I decided to show my face in the drawing room. I went there straightaway and opened the door, but since nobody noticed me I decided to watch for a moment… Nigel was at the window, you, Dr Grant, were in your armchair, and you, Helen, were by the fireplace. This was about twenty seconds before Nigel fell. I don't really know why I didn't own up right away. But when the police started questioning me I realised they suspected it was more than a mere accident, so I told myself that if I claimed to have entered the room at the very moment Nigel fell, I would have a perfect alibi. It was only afterwards that I realised how ridiculous it was, but by then I thought it was more prudent to stick to my original version of events.'

'Either way, your lie intrigued me greatly, Mr Holloway,' said Twist, adopting the air of a schoolteacher reprimanding a student for a minor offence. 'Of course I knew you weren't telling the truth, because I noticed your obvious embarrassment when my friend Hurst pointed out that you couldn't possibly confirm what Mrs Manson and Dr Grant were doing at the moment of the fall. You knew they were both innocent, but your hasty lie prevented you from saying so categorically... and that bothered you very much.'

The look that passed between Helen Manson and Frank Holloway did not escape Dr Twist's notice. He discreetly cleared his throat, then said, 'Which brings us to the final act. No doubt you all noticed Nathalie Marvel's strange behaviour after the tragedy. She seemed eager to leave the house as quickly as possible, but also eager to fulfil her civic duty by remaining until the investigation was complete. The truth was that she didn't want to miss out on any developments in the case. In a way, this proved beneficial – after all, if she hadn't stayed, she wouldn't have found out about the second photograph, which was a Sword of Damocles over her head. And that's why she ventured out to Victor Sitwell's house under cover of darkness and slipped a letter under his door. Incidentally, before I hand over the reins of this tale to Basil, I ought to note that the red silhouette witnessed by Mrs Crawford that night was most likely Nathalie Marvel, since she wore a red cloak.'

'A red cloak, yes, that's what I saw...' Basil commenced.

EPILOGUE

'WHO ON EARTH WAS IT? AND WHAT could they possibly want with Professor Sitwell at that hour? Those were the questions I asked myself when I saw her slipping something under the door...'

Basil Hawkins paused. That evening, he seemed like a different man as he held court, recounting the nocturnal adventures which had led him to save the professor's life. As for the professor himself, he'd recently been released from hospital and, apart from a few scratches and bruises, seemed to be in good shape. To celebrate, he had invited a few friends, colleagues, and other distinguished guests to dinner at a pleasant establishment in Tavistock – including Dr Twist and Inspector Hurst, with Basil as guest of honour. If not for Basil, he had said numerous times, there was no way he would have survived.

Basil was well-dressed – even distinguished. But the change in him was not merely sartorial; he had a new sense of confidence, and a boldness in his voice that would have been unthinkable even a week earlier. He positively shone among this crowd of luminaries, vaguely reminiscent of a jester entertaining the royal court after a feast. He had been invited to tell his side of the story, and complied without hesitation.

Ever since his protégé had begun to speak, Victor Sitwell had been casting curious glances at the large, mysterious package

Basil had brought with him. It was obviously a surprise – a gift? But what sort of surprise? What gift?

'I was intrigued, so I decided to follow that red silhouette. The fog was so thick that I eventually lost sight of her, but not before a light in a nearby window gave me a quick glimpse of her face… It was a face I recognised, though I couldn't quite place it.

'So, I retraced my steps to retrieve the envelope I'd seen her slipping under Professor Sitwell's door. It was a letter, asking him to meet the following night, around midnight, at the top of Wish Tor. And it was signed "Dr Twist", who is present here this evening, and who surely requires no introduction…'

There was a round of applause, which the eminent detective accepted modestly.

Basil continued, 'According to this letter, Dr Twist requested the presence of Professor Sitwell because he wanted his opinion on a theory as to the murder method – indeed, he wanted him to witness a demonstration which could only be carried out at the scene of one of the crimes. This rendezvous, the letter said, must take place under conditions of absolute secrecy, since the inspector – who disagreed with the theory – wouldn't approve of such a demonstration. In a postscript, "Dr Twist" requested that the professor bring with him the famous photograph…

'That was all the letter had to say, which naturally intrigued me a great deal – particularly since the supposed signatory hadn't actually delivered it himself. I spent a while wondering about this, trying to understand, and unwilling to discuss it with either the professor or Dr Twist for fear that I had got it wrong somehow.

'The following night, I kept lookout near the path to Wish Tor. That time, I got a better look at the face of the figure in red. And I knew then from the expression on that face that the individual in question had some malicious plan in mind. And as the figure moved away, an image flashed in my mind: the face of Annie Crook. That's when I realised the two faces were one and the same.

'When Professor Sitwell passed by a few minutes later, I was still in shock. But I managed to pull myself together when I realised she had evil designs on this great man.'

Victor Sitwell, blushing with pride, raised his hand to ward off the barrage of compliments, but Basil was already pressing on with the story. 'Before heading up to Wish Tor myself, I thought it prudent to try and warn the detectives, since I could see them silhouetted in the window across the street – I was in the doorway of Tom the carpenter's shop. I grabbed a bit of newspaper and a pencil, wrote a quick message and hurled it at the window. And then I headed up to the Tor.

'I got a bit lost and ended up on the eastern slope. Fortunately, I wasn't the only one who was deceived by the fog – the figure in red had obviously *intended* to push Professor Sitwell over the edge and into the stream. But, in fact, he fell a little way from the water, dropping right by me so I was able to grab his coat collar and pull him to safety. He'd hit his head on the way down, so he was unconscious. I quickly hoisted him over my shoulder and carried him down to Dr Grant's surgery, where the good doctor took excellent care of him.'

Basil thanked his audience with a nod, and then sat down to the sound of thunderous applause.

It fell to Dr Twist to make the closing remarks. 'Of course, Hurst and I did not know at the time that those footsteps in the fog were Basil's. Nathalie Marvel's quick thinking when she glimpsed us heading up to the summit of the Tor was admirable – more than worthy of the great actress she was. She found herself in a situation all the more desperate because she believed Professor Sitwell was dead, and that the discovery of his body would obviously incriminate her. So, she decided to re-enact a scene from ten years prior: that of a naïve young girl lured to her fate by an invisible man. And she didn't hesitate to hurl herself from the edge of the stage and into the orchestra pit, as it were – at a carefully chosen spot, of course. She calculated that if we discovered Sitwell's corpse, we would conclude that *he* had been the invisible aggressor who simply overbalanced when pushing her.'

After Dr Twist, it was Sitwell's turn to speak. He didn't skimp on superlatives in his speech, which was entirely devoted to the great and heroic Basil. He ended on a poignant note. 'Basil, I owe you my life.'

Another round of applause, at the end of which Basil stood. But instead of yet more thanks, he said something very strange. 'Now we're even.'

There was a moment of awkward hesitation, with the guests glancing between Basil and the professor, whose expression was one of surprise and incomprehension. With that, Basil seized the large package and ripped it open, before emptying its contents onto the white tablecloth.

'Roses…' said the professor. 'Roses, but… they look like…'

'Yes – they are indeed yours,' said Basil. 'I couldn't bring all of them, but I promise you now that there are none left in your garden. I cut every single one.'

The professor's face reddened and his eyes bulged. He tugged frantically at his shirt collar.

'I thank you, Professor Sitwell, for the bed of hay you provided for me, and for the exorbitant salary you paid me for my modest labours in your garden. I also thank you, on behalf of the whole village, for your gracious gift of a ten-shilling note in the collection plate every Sunday. An act of generosity which, I'm sure, you intended to be used solely for charitable works within the parish, and not to burnish your already-angelic reputation. That reputation which you have cultivated thanks to all your hard work. Hard work undertaken with a single goal in mind: the acquisition of goods and property.

'This reputation of yours has only improved since you met me, and since you – out of the goodness of your heart – befriended the poor itinerant drunkard I had become. Finally, I'd like to thank you on behalf of everyone you have personally rescued or helped over the years – like the gypsies you held in such high esteem, and for whom your refurbished barn by the river simply wasn't good enough. On behalf of them all, Professor Sitwell, I thank you one last time, and leave you to your roses.'

'Shall we make a bet, Hurst? I'll bet that it won't be long till Frank Holloway proposes to Helen Manson. And what's more, I'd be very surprised if she said no. I'll even go a step further: I think he'll make her very happy. What is my prediction based on? Experience. Oh, don't give me that look. Just because I'm a confirmed bachelor doesn't mean I don't know about these things. True, he isn't exactly a saint, but I think he's getting tired of show business, and is starting to like the idea of a "normal life", if you know what I mean.'

Inspector Archibald Hurst, who sat behind the wheel of his Talbot driving the pair back to London, heaved a long sigh, then said, 'If you don't mind, Twist, can we talk about something else? Like that very strange party last night. Poor Sitwell, surrounded by dead roses, and nobody knew if he was crying out of sorrow, spite or shame… what on earth got into Basil, do you think?'

'Can't you guess?'

'Guess what?'

'Tell me, Archibald, didn't you wonder *why* Basil was keeping lookout near the professor's house? And don't forget his sudden departure from the inn the previous day – can you recall what we were discussing at the time? Ah, but of course, you couldn't have known. You didn't know Basil's father. While I wouldn't call him a personal friend, I did have the opportunity to meet him several times. He was a decent chap. And I knew that Basil's face reminded me of someone. You see, when it comes to physiognomy I…'

'Get to the point, Twist, or I swear I'll drive us into a ditch.'

'All right, all right. Basil was the only son of the owner of a tin mine near Bodmin, who shot himself following a prolonged miners' strike. A strike which was instigated by Sitwell.'

'Good lord! But…'

'Yes. Do you see now why he reacted as he did when Sitwell himself told us about it? He realised he was sitting with the man who was directly responsible for the greatest tragedy of his life – a man he had previously considered a saint! He was about fifteen when his father killed himself. His mother did not last much longer, and Basil was taken in by their former gardener. He eventually joined the Navy when he came of age, and when he returned to civilian life he began his descent into alcoholic vagrancy.

'What he was *really* planning to do that night, while he was waiting outside the Sitwell house, was to seek revenge. He didn't know how exactly. But then he saw that red silhouette, and read the letter, and this briefly tempered his fury. The following night, he didn't hesitate to save the life of the man who had plunged him into misfortune and penury.'

For quite a long while, the inspector ruminated on this startling revelation, his brows furrowed and his hair dishevelled. Then he commented slyly, 'Now that I think about it, Twist, you did spend rather a long time talking to Basil over the last couple of days – in the run-up to his big moment at the party. You didn't have anything to do with that, did you?'

'Not at all, not at all,' said Twist, coughing awkwardly. 'Goodness, I spent most of the time trying to calm him down. You see, even though he had saved the professor's life, he was still keen to teach him a lesson he wouldn't soon forget…'

'You suggested a more subtle revenge, didn't you?'

'Well, it's true that I opened his eyes to Victor Sitwell's real nature.'

'And the roses were your idea?'

'They were so beautiful, and so at odds with the more treacherous aspects of the professor's personality. As he so often says, "the important thing in life is to be consistent in your behaviour". His love for the roses was his one inconsistency.'

'And that grand speech of Basil's – you wrote it for him, didn't you?'

Twist smiled, but did not reply.

About the Author

Photo courtesy of Paul Halter

Paul Halter is a French crime writer, known for his locked room mysteries.

His first published novel, *La Quatrieme Porte* (*The Fourth Door*), was published in 1988 and won the Prix de Cognac, given for detective literature. The following year, his novel *Le Brouillard Rouge* (*Red Mist*) won the Prix du Roman d'Aventures.